Also by the Author

THE FIRST WINSTON & CHURCHILL COLLECTION

SUMMER OF MISSING

THACHER E. CLEVELAND

FIRST PRINT EDITION

ISBN: 978-1545332078

For my Dad

Table of Contents

Never Let Go

May

"When you said we were going to fight evil, I didn't think that meant going to Queens," Lexie said, drumming her fingers on the dashboard of the '76 Gremlin that served as their company car.

"We go where the work is," Henry said. "And we don't even know if we're going to be doing any . . . 'evil fighting.' Did I even say that? It's a bit simplistic."

"It was implied. Not that I'm complaining or anything

but it's been about six months since we've seen anything of the demons and monsters brand of evil."

"True, but I know I said that those sort of cases weren't going to be an everyday occurrence. The mundane side of private investigation pays the bills, even if it's not as exciting as the extraordinary one," he said.

"So which is this?" Lexie said, nodding towards the house they were parked half a block away from. "Mundane or extraordinary?"

"I guess we'll have to wait and see."

"You don't even have a guess?"

He gave a little smile and checked his watch. "Looks like it's about time. He should be ready for us."

"You are such a tease," she said, getting out.

It was early in the afternoon, overcast and predictably quiet for a weekday. The neighborhood was almost nice despite the houses being pressed uncomfortably close together. Lexie heard a dog barking wildly, and as they got closer she saw it was a small mutt in the glassed-in porch of one of the neighbors. It stood on its hind legs, barking at the house Henry had pointed out with all the force it could muster.

When they got to the front gate of the house Henry

took out a small notebook, read his notes over, and then dropped it back into the pocket of his rumpled suit. He nodded at Lexie and the two of them opened the gate, headed through the tiny front yard and up the steps. Before they even got to the top the door opened and a small, middle-aged man stared at them through the screen door. "Small" was generous, as he barely scraped five feet tall and then slouched down and managed to lose an inch or two.

"Are you from the detective agency?" he asked them, his voice lowering to a whisper at the last bit.

"Yes, Mr. Chalmers." Henry said. "I'm Henry Churchill, we spoke on the phone. This is my associate, Lexie Winston."

The man nodded and opened the screen door for them. "Call me David, please." He motioned them through the foyer and into the living room, watching them nervously. Lexie had become accustomed to people's surprise at what an odd pair the two of them made. Her being tall, pale, and skinny, with long dark hair pulled into a ponytail through the back of her Knicks cap contrasted with Henry's shorter, rounder, dark-skinned body, his receding hairline and close-trimmed beard.

"Can I take your coats?" David asked.

Henry handed over his overcoat but Lexie waved him off, not wanting to make the already nervous man moreso by showing the Walther holstered at the small of her back. "I'll be right back with some refreshments," David said. The investigators stepped into a living room filled with plastic-covered furniture and halfdead plants and dotted with photographs. On the mantle of the decorative fireplace was a small colony of ceramic figurines, and before she could make a comment about them Henry shook his head at her.

"You never let me have any fun," she said. She wandered around the room, taking a closer look at the photos that dominated the far wall. There were a variety of pictures of David and a woman that must have been his wife at obvious vacation spots like the Grand Canyon, Mount Rushmore, and various family gatherings. The two smiled thinly or not at all as they leaned against each other. For a couple that didn't seem to like having their pictures taken, they sure had a lot of them. Looking closer, she could see that there were slightly lighter rectangular spots on the wall, some partially obscured by other pictures but all picture-sized.

"Thank you for coming all this way to see me," David said, coming into the living room holding a tray with a tea kettle, cups, and fancy cookies.

"It's no bother," Henry said. David set the tray on the table and sat across from them, folding his hands into his lap and almost disappearing into the soft cushions of the chair.

"You said that you were worried about your wife, that she'd been acting peculiar the past several months," Henry said.

David nodded. "Maybe it's nothing, I don't know. I could be overreacting but . . . I just get the feeling that something has happened to Mimi. She's different."

"In what way?" Lexie said, sitting down next to Henry.

"She keeps odd hours. She's been staying down in her workshop in the cellar whenever she's at home and for much later at night than she used to." He'd picked up one of the cookies and was just twirling it absently in his hand. "Several months ago she took almost a thousand dollars in cash out of the bank and wouldn't tell me what it was for. She's distant and doesn't really talk to me anymore."

"What do you think it is?" Henry asked.

"It's hard to say. Last year we lost our son, Conrad. She took it very hard."

"It's never easy to lose a child," Henry said.

"Do you have any of your own Mr. Churchill?"

"Two," Henry said. "Fourteen and sixteen."

David turned and looked at Lexie, who froze with a cookie halfway to her mouth. "No," she said. "Not really a breeder."

David's face crinkled up at her choice of words but he continued. "Conceiving was long and difficult and when it finally happened we were very, very grateful. We loved him and tried to take such good care of him, but when he was six there was an accident. He and Mimi were walking to the store and there was a drunk driver. Connie had been lagging behind, I guess, and Mimi was holding his hand." He stopped his fiddling and placed the cookie back on the tray with a trembling hand. "She turned back to scold him when the car came and just . . . ripped him right from her grip. The driver got a block further before he lost control and hit a bus. Both he and Connie were killed ."

David paused, looking over at the wall of photos and blinking away tears. "The year after his death was very hard on us both, but it seemed like things were slowly getting better. Then, right around his birthday she had a bit of a . . . well, I guess you'd call it a relapse. She started going on medication and at first I didn't think it was working but then things changed. She started feeling much better, but that's when her odd behavior started. "

"Is that around the time she took out the money?" Lexie asked.

He nodded. "We'd hardly ever fought about the finances, but that was all of our savings. That, along with her odd behavior, has made things very tense between us. I'm just not sure what else I can do."

"Anything else out of the ordinary?" Henry asked.

David opened his mouth to say something, but then closed it. The three of them were silent for several moments before he continued. "We were at a funeral for her uncle several weeks ago and as soon as we got to the church she said she smelled something horrible. After a couple of minutes she said she started getting some kind of rash, and it finally got so bad I thought she'd been burned or had some kind of allergic reaction."

Henry leaned back, running a hand over the short graying hair on his head.

"Did the rash go away by the time you got home?" he asked.

"Yes," David said. "She said it was just the sweater she

was wearing, but I've never seen something flare up like that and then go away so quickly. I don't even think she's allergic to anything."

"Was she baptized into that church?" Henry asked.

"Yes. Is that important?"

"It could mean a lot of things. David . . . you found something, didn't you? Something that made you want to call us because you couldn't really understand it, right?"

"Yes," David said. He looked from Lexie to Henry and back again, rubbing his hands together. "Your ad said that you handle the unusual and I found . . . something last week. I thought it was nothing at first, but then it . . . " he trailed off.

"Why don't you just show us?" Lexie said.

"It's upstairs," David said, getting up and waving them towards the narrow staircase near the front door. They followed him up the steps, past another army of portraits of friends and family lining the wall. She and Henry followed David past what looked to be his and Mimi's bedroom and stopped at the door at the end of the hall.

"This was Conrad's room," he said. His hand reached out for the doorknob but only hovered over it for a moment, trembling slightly. "We hadn't touched it after the accident, but after everything that had been happening recently I wanted to see it. I waited until she went to do her volunteering at the homeless shelter and that's when I found it."

He opened the door and waved them in. Lexie didn't know what she expected but it wasn't for the room to be mostly bare with more negative silhouettes on the wall where posters and pictures once hung. There were a couple boxes in the corner, a bed and a desk, but other than that the room was empty. Even the bed had been stripped of sheets and pillows, and with the small closet door ajar, all she could see were empty hangers.

"I don't know how long it's been like this," David said, his voice cracking. "I tried talking about cleaning his room a couple months after it happened but she screamed at me. She said I was trying to get rid of him, and now . . . "

"What else did you find?" Henry said, stepping into the center of the room and turning slowly to take it all in.

David walked over to the bed and got down on one knee. "I didn't want to move it in case she came looking for it, which is why I wanted you to come out here instead of me going to your office." After reaching around blindly for a moment, David's eyes widened and he pulled a bundle of cloth out from under the bed, setting it between him and Henry.

"Don't," Henry said as David went to unwrap it. David nodded and got back to his feet, letting out the breath he'd been holding. Henry bent over and picked it up, shaking his head at Lexie's smirk when he let out a grunt of exertion. Henry put the bundle on the desk and pulled at the corners of the cloth. It was a book, old and leather, with symbols etched on a cover practically black with age. As soon as it was uncovered Lex, could feel the air in the room change, become heavier and warmer .

"Looks like we're going with extraordinary," Lexie muttered.

"I was right, wasn't I?" David asked. "It's not normal, is it?"

"You could say that," Henry said, running a couple of fingers over the cover and leaning in to get a closer look. The book itself wasn't very thick but the cover was. The ornate swirls and symbols looked to have been pounded into the leather, but there were also scratches all over it. One of the corners even looked like something had chewed on it.

"When I realized the room had been emptied I just started looking all over the place, trying to see if she had just hidden Conrad's things somewhere, and that's when I found it. I wanted to open it to see what it was but I just couldn't bring myself to touch it anymore. That night I swore I could feel it down the hall. Like there was a pressure on my chest." As he spoke David's breath got shallower and he began to clutch at the front of his sweater.

"Okay, why don't we have a little breather," Lexie said, taking him by the arm and gently pulling him out of the room. He didn't resist, which was helpful, because despite the fact that she was pretty sure she could toss him down the hallway without too much effort, she felt that wasn't an approved method for handling a client.

"Good idea," murmured Henry, still staring down at the book.

Lexie got David turned around and headed towards the stairs, and once he was out of earshot she leaned back into the room.

"Should I be worried?" she asked.

"Moderately."

"Right," she said, turning and heading down the hall. "Situation normal, then."

She found David sitting in the kitchen, still clutching his sweater with one hand and holding an inhaler just as tight in the other. "I'm sorry," he said as she sat down. "I just can't believe that she would have something like that right where our son slept."

"Yeah," Lexie said. "It's pretty fucked up." He looked over at her with a face scrunched up in distaste and she realized she probably just deflowered the Chalmers' family kitchen. It was far too cute and too filled with lace and cartoon renderings of stereotypical Italians for that kind of language. There was one thing that stood out to her as she took in the quaint family kitchen and she crossed the room to the door opposite to get a closer look at it.

"Is this new?" she said, pointing to the shiny silver padlock just above the doorknob.

"Yes," David said. "That door leads down to the basement. Mimi had an extra lock put in a couple months ago."

"Why?"

David paused, trying to recall. "There's a storm door down there that leads outside and she was afraid someone would break in through there and get into the house." Lexie looked around, and then pointed at the door in the back of the kitchen that led out to the screened-in back porch. "If she was so worried about a break in, why didn't she want to have the screens back there replaced with glass?"

David looked from her to the porch and then back again. "I don't know. We never talked about that."

"And this is where you said she's been spending most of her time, right?"

"Yes," David said, turning his inhaler around and around in his hand.

"Do you have a key?"

His hand squeezed the fabric of his sweater again. "No." He took a deep breath to try to help the words come out, and they did. Quietly. "She said I didn't need one."

"Right," Lexie said, turning and examining the clasp and lock. "Do you have a screwdriver? Phillips-Head?"

He nodded and got up, heading into the living room and coming back moments later with the tool. One by one she removed the screws holding the clasp to the door, leaving it and the padlock dangling from the side screwed into the door jamb. "Voila," she said, opening the basement door. She flipped on the light switch, illuminating the stairwell. It curved down and around a corner at the bottom. Lexie strained to try to hear anything, and after a couple moments of silence she took a couple steps down.

"Is this new also?" she asked, tapping the nearly identical silver padlock and latch hanging open on the inside of the door. David nodded. "Okay. I want you to go upstairs and wait for me. I'm going to go and check it out." David nodded again, taking another look at the most recent evidence of his wife's heightened privacy concerns before heading upstairs. Once he was out of sight, Lexie drew her Walther, checked the clip, chambered a round and thumbed off the safety. She took the stairs as quietly as she could, trying to convince herself that she was being overly cautious.

Then again, why would Mimi Chalmers have locks on both sides of the door unless there was something that she wanted to make sure didn't get out even while she was down here?

A faint scent of artificial pine wafted up to her as she walked down the steps. When she reached the bottom and turned the corner the pine smell threatened to overwhelm her. A short hallway led to a darkened doorway and hanging from the ceiling and along the wall were dozens upon dozens of pine-scented car fresheners, some faded but others still bright and brimming with chemically-powered "freshness." Some hung so low she had to duck down to pass under them, and as she moved through the narrow hallway crammed with junk and cardboard boxes with precise labeling, the pine smell began to give way to one that was heavy, sour, and, unfortunately, familiar. She couldn't be sure, but Lexie had a fairly good idea that something down here was dead.

She hoped it stayed that way.

The small hallway opened into a darkened larger room and a bunch of air-fresheners hung in the doorway like a curtain. She brushed aside the fresheners and felt around the wall until she found the light switch. She turned it on and stood in the doorway, scanning the narrow room. The walls were paneled with fake wood and the floor covered in worn carpet, giving the place an underground office/bunker vibe. In the far corner there was a tiny desk with half-painted figurines and neatly lined up jars of paint. To her right was the storm door leading outside that Mimi had told her husband she'd been worried about. From where Lex stood she could see an interior padlock had been added to this door as well. In the corner opposite Mimi's workspace there was another doorway, this one with a blanket hanging from the ceiling like a makeshift door.

Lex crossed to it, stepping lightly and leading with her Walther. She put a hand on the blanket and drew it back a little. The rotting smell was stronger here and she waited until she acclimated to it. After a couple of moments she pushed the blanket open along the clothesline that had been strung up.

David wouldn't have had far to look for his son's missing things. They were laid out in the unfinished utility room in what Lex could only assume was a close replica of how his room upstairs had looked when he was alive. Toys were scattered on the superhero rug that covered the stone floor and the unfinished walls were veiled with old hanging sheets. All of the pictures of Conrad with his family missing from upstairs were displayed down here, hooked into the bedclothes-turned-wallpaper and hanging on nearly every wall of the small room as well as leaning against boxes that had been stacked in front of the furnace and water heater at the back of the room.

As she looked at them she realized Conrad was a cuter kid than Lexie thought his parents were capable of producing. Unlike the photos upstairs, every picture with their child showed David and Mimi big genuine smiles. The pictures seemed to be arranged roughly in chronological order, with a swaddled and happy baby Conrad on one side of the wall and a beaming, energetic six year old at an amusement park pulling his father towards a roller coaster on the other.

Against the wall at the end of the photographic tour of the short life of Conrad Chalmers was an old chest freezer, about three feet high and five feet long. She walked over, keeping her gun trained on it and trying to move without a sound as she stepped around Matchbox cars and action figures. The soft hum it gave off let her know it was still working, but she could also tell that it was the source of the rotting stench. She held her breath and lifted the lid. The sudden burst of cold, rancid air made her eyes water. She had to turn away to try to get some fresh air and almost let the lid drop back down. She'd half expected something to spring out at her and if it had it would've caught her at a disadvantage.

After a couple of seconds she turned back, breathing through her mouth to try to avoid the stench. Lying in the refrigerator on a bed of ice was a man staring up at her with dead, glassy eyes and a blackish-purple ring of bruises around his neck. His legs had been bent up to make him fit and his arms were crossed over his chest, giving him an almost fetal appearance. His shoulder-length hair was mostly frozen to his gaunt face and unkempt beard and he wore a tattered corduroy shirt over an even dirtier t-shirt but that was all; from the waist down he was naked.

He wore a makeshift diaper of plastic wrap with more wrapped around one of his calves as well. Lexie poked at it tentatively with her gun and it crinkled, leaving a dent that showed a deep black underneath not unlike the bruising around his neck. Bits of him covered by the diaper showed swaths of blood-black as well, including a large patch where his genitals would be. As she prodded him with the pistol, moving him slightly, a large cleaver clattered free from its resting place next to the man and slid down along the ice.

Lex let the lid close and turned away. "Jesus," she muttered, letting out a breath. She wasn't sure what she'd expected to find in Mimi's secret playroom/museum to her dead child, but it certainly wasn't the partially-butchered body of a strangled transient.

Something rattled behind her and she turned, snapping the Walther up. The sound came from the other side of the blanket covering the boxes and junk at the far end of the room. She waited and it came again, louder this time, like something metal shifting back and forth. As she stepped closer she could hear something else as well, a sort of high-pitched whine to match the shaking.

She was so intent on keeping her eyes forward that she kicked a small ball, which bounced off of one of the toys and hit where the blanket touched the ground. At the sound of the ball the shaking stopped and then started up again even stronger. The whine turned into angry little grunts and she could see something pushing against the other side of the blanket.

"Fuck this," Lexie said, yanking the blanket down and stepping back, pistol up and at the ready.

There was a crash of metal hitting concrete as something fell to the floor. It was a cage and the front of it had been caught on the blanket and toppled to the ground with her sudden tug. The four-foot square metal cage was probably designed to hold a small dog or cat, but whatever tumbled out of the door that popped open when it hit the ground was no animal.

It was about two feet tall with pale skin and an oversized, misshapen skull covered with sparse blond hair. It wasn't until it got to its feet, leaning to its right side on one leg that was shorter than the other, that she realized it was dressed in a child's clothes,. It shook off the shock of the fall and looked around the room, its back to Lexie. She stood perfectly still as it shuffled in place, turning its head from side to side as it tried to figure out what happened. It took two big steps, faster than Lex thought it could move, and then froze in its tracks. The bulbous head whipped around towards her and for a second she could see the little boy in the photographs that dominated the room, but when the motion stopped the only resemblance she could see was in the oversized blue eye staring at her.

The rest of the thing looked like someone had taken one of the pictures of Conrad Chalmers on the wall and tossed it in a fire. Cheerful innocence and charm had been melted, twisted, and pasted to the swollen head in front of her. The other eye, dipped lower and off-center, was cloudy with a cataract but she could tell it was green, not blue. There were a pair of dark freckles just below it that would look charming on a small child but on this thing looked like two sores. None of the pictures of Conrad had shown him with freckles, Lex realized, but there was something familiar about it, especially combined with the milky eye and the cleft in the thing's chin.

"Shit," she muttered. They looked familiar because she'd just seen them in the cooler, looking back up at her from a dead man's face.

At the sound she made the thing snarled at her and

darted forward on uneven legs. Lex swung a foot up just in time for it to run into her boot and get kicked away. It hit the ground and rolled on its side, mewling for a second like an injured animal and then flipping itself over on all fours with a wicked hiss. Its legs were tiny and one of its arms even more so, but the other arm was swollen and as monstrously disproportionate as the thing's head.

Lex raised her gun but before she could get a shot off the thing launched itself into the air and onto one of the ledges holding photographs. It clung to the sheet covering the wall with its scrawny arm and grabbed a picture of Conrad and his mother sitting in a park and beaming at the camera. She ducked just in time for the photo to sail over her head before smashing into the wall behind her.

"Fine," Lex said. "Let's play." She raised the Walther and fired twice as the thing pulled itself along the wall by the sheet, sending pictures crashing to the ground in its wake. It was as fast as it was malformed and she couldn't get a bead on it, missing both times.

When it came to the corner of the room it leaped up to the ceiling to grab one of the pipes. Lex hesitated, not wanting to shoot something dangerous or put a round through the kitchen floor and perhaps hit David. The hesitation cost her. The thing swung down at her from the ceiling, landed about four feet away and grabbed a large metal truck from the ground with its mammoth paw. It hurled the toy at her, and it bounced off her forehead with a surprising force that made her vision blur. She could see the thing leap up at her again and she fired blindly at it.

The thing slammed into her chest, knocking the wind out of her and the gun from her hand before toppling her over. The back of her head hit the hard cement with tooth-rattling force. It grabbed her throat with its muscular hand and when she tried to get to her feet it slammed her head back down to the ground. The brilliant blue eye filled her vision as the little monster pressed down on her, breath ripe with rotted meat. The smell didn't last, as it was cutting off her air. As she felt herself begin to black out she wondered how much damage those needle-like teeth would do to her before Henry came to check on her.

Before it leaned in close enough for Lexie to find out for sure, the thing stopped and looked up. With her breath fading it took her a second to realize it was looking past her and at the hallway and stairway beyond. She made one final push to get up but she was driven back down again.

Just before she blacked out, she heard the sound of its little sharp nails clattering along the cement as it headed up towards freedom.

Henry flipped through the book, skimming through the passages he dared take a close look at and doing his best not to let any of the words linger for too long in his mind. Wherever the book had come from it was definitely authentic and certainly not the kind of thing you'd expect to find hidden away by a church-going, homeless-shelter-volunteering middle-aged woman.

Then again he'd seen worse in the homes of those that seemed better.

After reaching the end of the book he closed it, wrapped it in the cloth it had been found in, and tucked it under his arm. It was hard to tell what parts Mimi Chalmers had paid close attention to given its condition, but none of them were remotely safe or sane. The book centered on summoning rituals and not out-and-out necromancy, but there were some rites and ceremonies that might be appealing to someone desperate for the return of a lost child. Many required items or skills that would be nearly impossible for someone like Mimi to find; most required sacrifices or deeds that no sane person would consider.

All would leave an indelible stain on the soul, a stain so dark it could very well lead to madness.

Henry was halfway down the steps when he heard the muffled but unmistakable sound of gunshots, two in rapid succession. He took the rest of the stairs in two leaps and rounded the corner heading back to the kitchen as fast as he could despite the throbbing complaints from his bad knee that reminded him he wasn't twenty-five anymore.

Henry nearly ran into David as another shot came from below. David was heading out of the kitchen with his eyes wide and face just as white as when he recalled touching the book. Henry put a hand out to keep him from touching it again and tried to calm him down.

"What was that?" David said. "It sounded like gunshots, but--"

"Where's Lexie?" Henry said, leading him back into the kitchen.

"She went downstairs, into the basement. She was going to look and see if there was anything in Mimi's stuff down there that . . . " He trailed off. "What is that?"

Henry turned and saw the little thing skitter across the kitchen floor, pulling itself along with one oversized arm and manically kicking its tiny feet. It stopped and turned towards them at the sound of David's horrified whisper.

"David--" Henry started, trying to move him towards the hallway, but the thing leaped up on the counter and darted forward, swinging its arm and sending tiny little figurines and a handful of small dishes hurling towards them and cutting them off from the doorway.

"Back up, back up," Henry said, pushing David farther into the kitchen. Henry glanced over his shoulder and saw that there was a door leading out into the small backyard.

"What is that thing?" David said as it hurled a decorative bottle in their direction.

"It doesn't matter," Henry said, wanting to get David out and into the yard before it dawned on him what his wife had created. "I'm going to try to distract it and I want--"

The thing gave a yell and hopped off the counter, then bounded from the floor to the kitchen table in the center of the room and then to the counter closest to them. It swung at the toaster oven and sent it clattering across the counter, knocking over more things in its path, including a block of carving knives that spilled its contents across the counter.

Henry backed up more, pushing David farther behind him. The thing was much closer now and almost between them and the back door. "David, I want--"

"Conrad? Oh my god." David worked his way around Henry's arm faster than he'd thought possible. "Connie? What did she do to you?"

"It's not him," Henry said, trying to pull David back. He just shrugged the detective off, taking another step forward.

"My little boy . . . what did she do to my little boy?"

The thing Mimi made stopped for a moment, cocking its head at David.

"That's not your little boy," Henry said, stepping closer. "She used this book to make something unnatural and it only looks like your son." The thing hissed at Henry and then reached down for one of the small carving knives on the counter in front of it. It picked it up and threw it at Henry in one smooth motion.

Henry stepped back, the knife sailed through the space between him and David before hitting the wall.

"Stop it!" David snapped, turning to look at Henry.

"You're upsetting my son!"

"It's not--" The thing grabbed another knife, larger this time, and hurled it at David. Henry lunged forward, grabbing at David with one hand and extending the book with the other. There was a solid thunk as the knife buried itself in the book which was held right in front of David's face. Henry winced as his bad knee shuddered and then gave out, dropping him to the ground.

"Run!" Henry said through gritted teeth, rolling over onto his back as he tried to pry the knife from the book.

The thing hissed in anger again, picking up another large knife from the counter. David stood still as the thing took a step and then launched itself through the air. At the top of its arc it snapped to the side as a gunshot echoed through the kitchen. It hit the floor and bounced, splattering greyish green blood on the tile next to where Henry lay. The monster gave a shallow whine, its hand opening and closing on the handle of the knife. With a grunt of effort Henry yanked the knife from the book and rolled over, plunging it into the thing's milky dead eye. It gave a shudder and then stopped moving.

"Everyone okay?" Henry said as he pulled himself up from the floor.

"It hit me with a truck," Lexie said from the basement doorway, her voice hoarse and strained. "A toy truck," she clarified at Henry's quizzical look.

"You said . . . you said that thing wasn't my son." David said, rocking back and forth as if he was torn between wanting a closer look at the dead thing on his floor or backing away from it entirely.

"It's not. Your wife used information from that book to make something that was almost your son, that looked like parts of him, but it wasn't really him," Henry said, resting a hand on the man's shoulders and moving him away from the mess. The force David had shown before had left him, although Henry hoped it wasn't for good.

"I don't want to alarm anybody," Lexie said, taking a seat at the kitchen table. "But there's a dead body in the basement."

That shook David from his daze as he sat at the table across from her. "What? How?"

Henry cleared his throat and shot Lex a hard glare before turning his attention back to David. "There are things she needed to do to create that thing and that was probably one of them. What we need to do now is get ready for when the police arrive and figure out what we can tell them and what we can't."

"Oh god," he said, putting his face in his hands. "We just wanted a family. We just wanted our little boy."

They gave David a moment and then moved him into the living room while they cleaned up the kitchen.

"What are we going to tell the police?" Lexie asked, her voice a little stronger now.

"The truth."

She raised an eyebrow. "Well, just the parts they'll believe," he said, picking up the tiny, foul-smelling body and dropping it into the trash bag that Lexie held away from herself as far as possible.

"What the hell is that thing anyway?" she asked.

"A homunculus." When he saw her pause in tying up the bag and just stare at him he continued. "It's an artificial person created through black magic, normally made to do its master's bidding."

"Normally?"

"Well, whatever passes for normal for those that enjoy making things that involve the semen of a strangled man, blood, and manure."

"Jesus, no wonder it smells so bad. How'd she get it to look like their son?"

"The creature takes on the appearance of whatever is used to make it. In addition to the semen from the man that I'm assuming was strangled, she probably added some of Conrad's hair that they had."

"Fantastic. So now what?"

"Now we call the police and tell them we found a dead body. Hopefully before any of the neighbors have called to report gunshots."

She frowned at that. "Okay, smart guy, if we're not mentioning junior here, how are we accounting for the shots fired?"

"I'll take care of it."

"Oh really?" She walked over and pointed at the small hole in the kitchen wall where the bullet that felled the creature ended up. "Did you bring some spackle and matching wallpaper?"

He walked over, closed his eyes and placed his palm over the hole. His lips moved but he made no sound. After almost a minute, he took his hand off the wall which now appeared completely undamaged. "Souvenir," he said as he dropped the mashed bullet into her outstretched palm. "I'm going to get the ones downstairs."

"Show off," she called after him, tossing the bullet into the bag with the creature.

Henry came back upstairs with two more bullets to go into the bag and then carried it out to the car.

"What if the neighbors see? Mysterious black guy carrying a trash bag to his car right before the police arrive? Kind of suspicious." Lexie leaned against the counter, her arms crossed over her chest.

"First of all, there's no need for profiling. Second of all they aren't going to see. Even the ones that may be looking. Just stay here and have him call this in."

"What do I say?" David asked after Henry left.

"The truth. You were worried about your wife so you called us to look into it. We discovered a dead body and now we're calling the police. You didn't do anything wrong."

"Do you think they'll believe that?" he said, staring at the phone in his hand as Henry returned

"I hope so. Don't worry, we'll take care of you." Henry

took out his wallet and handed David a card. "This is my wife's number. She's a lawyer and used to helping people out of situations like this. She'll make sure that you're okay."

He paused, fingers just over the buttons. "What about Mimi?"

Lex held her breath for a moment and then let it out. "I don't think there's anything anyone can do for her. It's going to be pretty clear what she did and she's going to have to pay for it."

"I know. I just . . . " he trailed off, turning the phone over and over in his hands. Lex reached out and held it still. He nodded and dialed the numbers.

"Hello? Yes, hi . . . I . . . my name is David Chalmers and there's a dead body in my house."

Mimi Chalmers came home an hour later.

The police had showed up about ten minutes after David got off the phone and about twenty minutes after that a forensics team and the coroner arrived. Lex had gone over her statement twice by that point and wasn't relishing a third, so she was almost grateful for the interruption.

The coroner was in the process of taking the body out

the front door when they heard one of the officers outside call out, "Hey, you can't go in there!" David got to his feet quickly and Myers, the detective that was questioning him, followed. "Mr. Chalmers, wait!" Lex and Henry followed them onto the porch.

Lex recognized Mimi from the pictures in the basement, even though she bore no current resemblance to the smiling, plump, and photogenic middle-aged mother in them. Mimi's hair trailed behind her in a frantic, frizzy wave as she raced down the sidewalk, shrugging off the grasp of the patrolwoman she'd forced her way past. When she saw the sheet-covered body being lowered down the steps she let out a shriek and ran even faster towards her front gate.

"My baby! What have you done with my baby?"

"Mrs. Chalmers, stop!" Myers said, squeezing past the gurney on the steps and trying to intercept her.

"Where is he? Where is my baby boy?" she yelled again, her voice rising to a panicked scream. The two met just outside the gate, with the female officer right behind her. Myers put a hand up to try to slow her down but she slapped it away. Myers' other hand went down to his belt, but she crashed past him before he could draw his sidearm, knocking him to the ground in the process.

"What did you do?" Mimi screamed as she opened the gate, finally seeing David on the porch. "What did you do to my baby? Where is he?" The officer finally caught up to Mimi and grabbed her by the arm, yanking Mimi back before she could make it to the steps. Mimi turned and swung at her, but the patrolwoman ducked and twisted around behind her, bending Mimi's arm backwards.

David winced, and Henry put a hand on his shoulder. Lexie wasn't sure if it was to comfort him or to make sure he didn't try to help his wife.

"No! No!" Mimi screamed as the officer twisted her arm up behind her. "Where is my baby? What did you do? What did you do to my baby?" The officer was struggling to keep Mimi from breaking away, especially since Mimi outweighed the young woman by a good fifty pounds. Lex took a step forward to help but Myers, who had gotten to his feet all red-faced, raised his hand to wave her back.

"Mrs. Chalmers, you're under arrest," he said, trying to make himself heard over her screaming. She lunged forward, trying to get to the house but the patrolwoman holding her stood her ground. Myers grabbed Mimi's outstretched arm and the two of them tried to force her down. The patrolwoman stepped behind Mimi's knee, driving it and her to the ground.

"Stop resisting!" Myers grunted, trying to pin her shoulder to the ground.

"David, come inside," Henry said, trying to get him back into the house. David wouldn't move.

"Connie! Connie, Mommy's here! It's going to be okay!" Mimi screamed as Myers and the patrolwoman finally got handcuffs on her. She continued to thrash and struggle and Myers placed his knee in her back to try to hold her still, yelling over her that she was under arrest and asking if she understood her rights.

"Connie where are you? Where's my baby?"

He nodded to the female officer, who stood and unclipped the pepper spray from her belt.

"Come on," Lex said, turning David back into the house. "You don't need to see this." He nodded, and they closed the door just as her screams turned from panic to pain.

Henry and Lexie were quiet most of the way back into Manhattan.

"So you've seen a book like that before, right?" she said.

"Ones like it, yeah. That one looked to be one of a kind."

"So I'm not wrong in thinking it's weird that a grieving mother just happened upon someone who was presumably selling this thing?"

"You are definitely not wrong."

It was quiet for a while again.

"Are you okay?" she asked.

"As well as can be expected."

"This is a parent thing, right?"

He nodded. "You said that I told you we were going to fight evil. I'm pretty sure I said we were going to help keep people from evil."

"There's a difference?"

"Between helping and fighting? Yeah, there is. We may have taken something bad out of the hands of someone who never should've had it and we may have killed an unnatural monster, but I don't think we helped anyone."

A Love Supreme

June

"Let's say I felt the need to shoot the computer. That'd be okay, right?"

Henry leaned his head through the doorway. "I'd rather you didn't."

Lexie glowered at him from behind what had been the receptionist's desk but was now just an empty workstation in the ten-foot-square reception area of their private investigation firm. There hadn't been a receptionist in the seven months she'd been working with Henry so it mostly went unused, but most of the bookkeeping files were on the neglected computer sitting on the tiny desk that faced the even smaller couch that was the room's only furniture. Aside from a wide-angle black-and-white framed photograph of downtown Manhattan, the room was quite sparse.

"You're aware this thing doesn't work, right?" she said, tapping impatiently at the keyboard.

"It could be that you don't know how to work it," he said, leaning back into their office.

"I'm pretty sure I know how to operate a computer, it's just that this one is a piece of crap. Can't we get a new one?"

"No. Would you like to switch with me and file case logs?"

She snorted. "No thanks. I don't know how you call that filing when we can't find anything in there. It's like your record keeping system was designed by bears. Wait, was it? Because that'd be pretty impressive for bears . . . and I think I'd understand it more."

There was silence from inside the office.

"Fine, but don't blame me if the entire bookkeeping history 'accidentally' gets deleted and we have to start over with something that, y'know, makes sense."

She worked in silence for a couple of moments until someone rapped on the glass door to their office. "Good," she muttered. "The bears have returned to trade administrative work for honey and fish." The knocking came again. "It's open!"

A portly middle-aged man pushed the door open and looked around with narrowed eyes, taking in everything so fast it made his shoulder length, tightly curled hair whisk audibly at the collar of the track suit that was slightly too small for him.

"This the detectives?" he said.

"Yes," she answered. "We are all the detectives."

"Great. Be a sweetheart and get Mr. Churchill for me, will ya doll?"

"Sure thing," she said, matching his accent and beginning to loudly chew non-existent gum. "Mistah Churchill," she bellowed into the office. "You gotsa visitah!"

Henry stepped out, high forehead creased with irritation. "I heard," he said, extending a hand to the oversized stereotype that towered over Henry's five-and-a-half-foot frame. "I'm Henry Churchill. This is my associate, Lexie Winston."

"Mike Morrison," the man said, taking Henry's hand and shrugging at Lexie. "Sorry, I thought you were the secretary."

"Of course you did," Lexie said, getting to her feet. "What else did you need help with?"

"It's my daughter. She's in trouble and I was told you could help."

"I hope we can," Henry said as he leed Mike into the office and turned back to glare at Lexie while she followed.

"What?" she said. "This is why I don't like sitting out there."

Just beyond the door was Lexie and Henry's office, which was a little over twice the size of the reception area. Half of it contained their two desks placed at right angles to each other and the half just inside the door was their conference area. Which was a fancy way to describe a pair of poorly-aged leather chairs, a sofa, and a coffee table between them.

Mike sat on the sofa, looking from the tall, pale and slender Lexie, who had her boots up on the table and fingers steepled at her chin, to the heavyset, black and middle-aged Henry who sat back in his chair, fingers laced across his chest.

The couch was small, but Mike made it look like doll furniture.

"I'm sorry about before," Mike said. "Jimmy Santini told me you were the person to see about stuff like this, but he didn't say anything about her," he noded in Lexie's direction.

"She's new," Lexie said.

"And very good at what we do," Henry said, turning slightly to scowl at her. "If Jimmy Santini told you to come and see me," Henry said, "then this must be something special."

"Yeah, you could say that," his curls bobbed up and down as he leaned forward, resting his elbows on his knees and rubbing his face roughly with a big paw of a hand. When he stopped a few moments later and looked up at them his eyes were pink and almost dry.

"My wife died from cancer a few years back," he said, clearing his throat. "Ever since I've tried to raise our daughter Marcia the best way I know how. I knew teenagers could be a handful, seeing as how I put my folks through hell, but a daughter's supposed to be different, y'know? As time went on I felt her just slipping away and nothing I did could get her back in line. She kept getting wilder and wilder and pretty soon all I could do was yell at her. She just barely graduated last spring and didn't have the grades for college. She didn't want to work so I kind of just let her coast, figuring she'd find her way eventually. After a while though, all she was doing was partying and it got to the point where I'd barely see her. Most of her friends were going to school so I figured this would end come September, but by then she had a whole new crowd to run with and there was no end in sight. For nearly a year she'd be just hanging around, partying. She had a couple of jobs but she screwed up all of them.

"About a month ago she came home after being gone for nearly three days. She doesn't say anything to me just starts packing her stuff. She says that she's got a new job and didn't need me anymore. At first I thought that maybe this was on the level but I could tell she just looked . . . wrong. I tried to stop her, and get her to tell me where she'd been but she wouldn't hear of it. I figured I'd give her some time to cool off and she'd come to her senses. It wasn't until after she left that I realized that she'd pinched my mother's good silverware and the wad of cash I keep for emergencies. Almost a thousand bucks."

"What do you mean looked wrong?" Henry said.

"She was real pale, nervous, kinda fidgety. She had bruises and there were marks on her wrist and neck. She was always careful about how she looked, and I've never seen her acting all . . . strung out. I didn't want to think drugs, but I don't know. After a couple of weeks I couldn't take it anymore so I took some time off work and started looking everywhere for her.

"One of her friends had seen her in some underground club in an old warehouse down in Red Hook, so I went there to bring her back home and straighten her out no matter what. Some tough guy I was, they wouldn't even let me in the front door. After standing on the sidewalk screaming at them to let me in they sent some guy out who said he'd take me to her.

"He took me up into one of the offices and this other guy was waiting for me. Black guy, dressed really nice, sitting in a big chair like a king with Marcia curled up next to him. It seemed like she wanted to get up and see me but he just reached down to pet her hair and she stopped moving. He was just staring at me, and then it was like . . . I couldn't move, couldn't even think. He was talking and I don't even remember what he said. I was just nodding and I was saying something too and then I was home and I had no idea how I had gotten there.

"I didn't even remember I had found Marcia until later that day. There was more, I know there was, but all I could remember were his eyes and his teeth. I thought . . . " he trailed off, he brow furrowed at the effort of remembering what little he did.

"You thought what, Mr. Morrison?"

"I think maybe he did something to me and I just can't remember. Or I don't want to remember. At first I just brushed it off, thinking I was just hurt because she didn't want anything to do with me, but it kept nagging at me. A couple days later I remembered almost everything and I knew I needed help. I went to the police and they just gave me some bullshit, but I couldn't let it go. I kept calling and bugging every cop I could find, but they were just full of shit."

"Except Jimmy Santini," Henry said.

"Yeah. He called me a day or two later and told me to come and see you, so here I am."

"You realize that she's eighteen and she's going to make her own decisions, don't you Mr. Morrison?" Lexie added.

"Yeah, but I don't think she's doing that anymore."

Henry just nodded. "You're right, she isn't. Which is why we're going to help you."

As soon as Mike left the office Lexie exclaimed, "Holy crap, is this a vampire?" Henry let out a deep sigh and nodded. "Well I'm sorry if this is old hat to you," she said. "Pardon me for being excited about going after one of the classics."

It turned out "going after" was a slow and deliberate process. The two drove out to Red Hook. Nestled among the abandoned and soon-to-be-renovated warehouses near the Brooklyn shore was the address Mike had given them. In the day it looked like nothing special but when the sun (and even the moon) went down small groups of well-dressed young people began to congregate near it. They'd wait for a few moments before a burly, thug-ish doorman poked his head out of the unmarked door and waved most of them in. Those that got overlooked, mostly young men whose "dates" were admitted, hung around until they were shooed away. While they didn't do much to conceal the club, they certainly didn't do anything to attract attention to it.

For almost two weeks the investigators sat in the schoolbus-yellow Gremlin and watched the place from various angles and distances. "There's something odd going on here," Henry said as they headed home.

"Really? There's something odd about a vampire in an

underground nightclub? Please, share." Lexie said.

"Did you notice the other men? The ones that looked out of place?"

She nodded. Every night there had been older men, nothing like what you'd expect a night club's clientele to be, wandering around the warehouse. They'd sometimes come to the club door and instead of being turned away they'd have a slightly longer conversation with the doorman before continuing on their way. Many of them nodded and then proceeded around the building. It took the detectives a couple of days to notice that there was a second entrance, near the back of the warehouse in an alleyway.

"So what do you think it is?" she asked.

"I don't know. It doesn't look like drugs, doesn't seem like they're there for the party scene."

Lexie interrupted with a derisive laugh. "'Party scene?' Really? Are there folks that are still looking for the party scene?"

"You know what I meant."

"Sure thing, daddy-o. I dig that swinging scene, man."

Henry let out a deep sigh. "Well, since we don't know what's really going on in there, I guess that means someone is going to have to go inside. Since I'm so unhip and all, I guess it'll have to be one of our other investigators. "

She sighed. "You suck, you know that right?"

"I have teenagers. I'm well aware of how much I suck," he said with a wry smile.

It took some dipping into the petty cash fund to get Lexie some clothes that allowed her to blend in with the club crowd, as well as a more liberal application of makeup than she'd ever been comfortable with. All in all that package made her feel like the most tarted up form of bait ever.

"I'm going to assume they aren't going to let me in with a gun in my bag, and I'm pretty sure I don't have any place I can conceal it," she said, looking down at herself. "I'd kind of like a little protection, if you know what I mean. Especially if I come face to face with a real bloodsucker."

Henry nodded. "I have some ideas about that. Especially if you run into a bloodsucker."

"So what's the plan here?" she said, stepping out of the high heels with a relieved sigh. "We're assuming there's only one vampire, but given how cautious you've been it makes me think that just one might be a bit much for us to handle."

"If all goes according to plan then we won't have to handle it at all. Just get in, find her, and then get the hell out," Henry said, going over his notes.

"Really?" she said, dropping down on the couch across from him. "There's an honest-to-god vampire out there and we aren't going to take it out? I have a feeling Marcia Morrison isn't his only victim."

"But she's the only one we're being paid to rescue. If we try something bigger, something more direct, and it goes badly there may be some blowback."

"And you think that's worth avoiding to the point of not making sure this thing can't keep using people like this?"

Henry closed his notebook. "I've been doing this for a long time. I'm not saying that to be condescending, but I just want you to understand that there are a lot of factors in play in this world we work in. Sometimes you have to tread carefully."

"And that means leaving behind girls just because we want to cover our own asses?"

He was quiet for a moment and then shook his head. "We'll see what happens."

It took a night, but Lexie finally made it in. After a

week of going there and scoping out the place, she began to consider suicide. Their instincts were right, there was something more going on than a bunch of blaring-loud computer sounds disguised as music playing to a mind-numbing light show. There wasn't much to the place aside from tables, a couple bars, and a DJ booth, all of which seemed to be easily transportable and most likely gone by dawn. After getting her bearings, Lexie could see that there was a balcony VIP area that seemed to be mostly populated by attractive, scantily-clad young women. If she looked closely she could see some men that looked like they'd fit in with the crowd being let in through the alleyway out back. More often than not, they'd hang out with their female companions for a little bit and then disappear through one of the doorways she could barely make out.

From what she could tell there was one way to get upstairs from the dance floor level ,but it was constantly guarded by a rotating host of burly men who made the ones working the door look downright friendly. Every now and again she'd see a young woman picked out of the crowd and led through the door. After that, she didn't see them again.

Despite Henry's protestations, she knew that was the easiest way to try to get behind the scenes and look for Marcia.

Of course, the only way she could think to do that made her skin crawl. She was drumming her fingers on the comically small handbag she'd been forced to carry when she saw the man that matched Mike's description of the guy who'd taken him up to the vampire's office. She'd caught glimpses of him before on the balcony but this was the first time she'd seen him on the club level. Her drumming paused as she watched him circulate around the periphery of the dance floor. He watched the action with a smug little smile. With a scowl she dug the phone out of her bag and texted Henry, who was still maintaining the watch about a block away.

I'm going in. Will try to exit out back. Keep an eye out.

She silenced her phone and then stuffed it back in the bag. She took a deep breath, put on her best fake smile, and strode towards her target. She let herself wobble a little in her heels, smiling even wider when he glanced over and made eye contact.

"Well hello there," he said, checking her out from mini skirt to artificially-constructed cleavage to hair wound up in a bun and held in place by a pair of chopsticks. "I'm Tony DiMarco," he said, extending a stubby hand poking out of an expensive shirt. The first two shirt buttons were undone and a trio of diamond and gold necklaces tried to signal for help as they drowned in a sea of chest hair. "I manage this club."

"I'm Staci," she said, shaking his hand and trying to smile through the fog of Drakkar Noir and cheap cigars. "With an 'I.'"

"Very, very nice to meet you, Staci-with-an-I. What can I do for you?"

"Well," she said, pulling herself closer to him, "I've only been here a couple of times but every time I've seen you and I could tell that you were the big man around here--"

"Oh, I'm big all right," he interrupted.

"You are so bad!" she squealed, slapping his arm. It took everything in her power to keep from doing it harder. And to his face. Until her hand got numb. "See, I knew you'd be the one to talk to around here. I mean, I've been trying to get up there," she nodded up towards the balcony, "but they're so mean they won't let me. I figured if I talked to you I'd be able to get into the real party."

"Oh you want the real party, huh?"

"Yes please," she said, drawing even closer to him.

"I think we can work something out. Come with me."

Tony led her to the door upstairs. The man guarding the door glared at them with tiny eyes nearly hidden under a

Neanderthal brow.

"Going up, Marco," Tony said, clapping the not-so-gentle giant on the arm. Marco grunted what might have been an affirmative.

They walked up the stairs to the balcony and when she turned towards the area where the so-called VIPs were lounging, Tony took her by the arm and gently but insistently pulled her in the opposite direction. "Not so fast, sweetheart. You wanted to see where the real party was, right?"

She nodded and followed him down to the other end of the balcony where another doorway and set of stairs waited for them. At the top was another Marco, this one smaller and Latin and named Carlos. He was so proud of that, in fact, that he had it in gold on a chain around his neck. Past Carlos was a hallway stretching in both directions for what appeared to be the length of the building with doors evenly spaced on both sides.

Tony led her to the right and as they passed some of the doors she could hear the sounds of almost comically over-exaggerated sex. When they got to the door at the end of the hall Tony unlocked it and held it open, waving her in with a greedy smirk on his face.

"Wow, this is big" she said, walking in and looking around at a room larger than her apartment. The wallpaper was a nearly neon red and in the center of the room was a colossal bed with matching red sheets. Polished black furniture dotted the rest of the suite, although she was sure that almost none of it got any use.

"Oh yes, we're much bigger than we appear."

"Is that a fact?" she said, looking over her shoulder at him and trying her best to will him into the room with her so she could beat some information out of him.

"Guilty as charged," he said, not moving from his spot in the open doorway. "However, there is something I have to attend to first," he said. "Wait right here for me and I'll be back with a little surprise for us."

"Hurry back," she said.

"Count on it," he said, closing the door. There was a slight jiggling of the handle and the sound of a bolt being thrown.

"Wonderful," she muttered, crossing her arms in irritation and beginning a slow walk around the room. No windows and no phone, not that she was expecting anything that easy. She reached into her bag to text Henry but before she could find her phone a voice whispered in her ear.

"Don't worry. He didn't leave you here alone."

Her body went rigid.

"I love it when he brings me something fresh to eat," the voice purred in her ear. An ebony hand reached across her and took ahold of her purse. "Let me get this out of your way."

Without being able to stop it, she let him take the purse and put it on the small table next to them. "There we go. Much better. Much easier to relax."

Henry had told her what to expect if she came face-to-face with this thing. He told her to focus, don't look it in the eyes, and try to keep her mind clear, but he hadn't said anything about the voice that was so deep and smooth it felt like it was sliding inside her brain and massaging away her thoughts.

It placed its hands on her shoulders and they were cold enough that it felt like he was drawing the heat right out of her. She couldn't feel any breath on her neck but she knew that it was just millimeters away from her exposed flesh. Everything from her toes to her upswept hair was electrified and her body shook with the sudden rush of adrenaline.

"You're scared."

She nodded.

"That's okay. Relax."

The adrenaline shakes stopped as soon as they had started.

"Much better."

Fingertips slid down her shoulders to her elbows, dragging fingernails along her flesh. It felt like sparks shot right into her chest.

"What's your name?"

"Alexis Marie Winston."

"Pretty." The nails went back up her arms, harder this time. She wanted to draw in breath from the shock of it but didn't know if that was allowed. When the hands reached her shoulders again they hooked fingernails under the thin straps of her blouse. There was a sudden intake of air and she realized that it was smelling her.

"Delicious. Take your hair down."

She reached up and took the chopsticks from her hair, letting it fall past her shoulders and brush against her face. There was something she should do, something she needed to do. It was at the tip of her mind.

"Put them on the table."

She put the sticks on the table.

"Turn around."

This was bad. This was unnatural. No one had ever made her insides feel this soft and warm before, but something was banging around inside her head trying to convince her this wasn't right. Turning around wasn't what she should be doing. Turning around wasn't--

"Turn around."

She turned around, keeping her gaze lowered. All she saw was the deep red of a silk shirt that matched the wallpaper, unbuttoned at the top and showing the same ebony as the hands that had played havoc on her arms.

"Look at me."

Her mind ran riot now, thoughts slammed together in her brain hard enough that she felt herself blinking uncontrollably. This was wrong.

"Look. At. Me."

She looked up at him. She could feel her brain trying to process his face and see what he looked like but she only saw the teeth, gleaming perfect white in stark contrast to his skin, and eyes so bloodred they couldn't possibly be human. Eyes that pulled her inside out with fear and desire.

"Let me taste you."

It leaned close and she felt an intake of air that wasn't breath but the sudden gasp of a predator about to strike. That sound brought back some of her senses and she realized that if she didn't act she was going to die. Slowly. Probably over many months. Focus, Henry had said. Focus and control.

She was in control. Not it. And she had . . . what did she have?

The teeth were pressing up against her throat and almost breaking the skin. Teeth. That's it.

She had teeth of her own.

She reached out at the table, trying see what she was grasping for out of the corner of her eye. She wasn't able to turn her head or move the rest of her body and she almost panicked when she couldn't find them but then she felt the smooth, engraved surface of her weapon. With all the strength she could muster she drew away from him until she could see the bright teeth and bloodred eyes.

Recognizing her best target, she grasped the chopstick and plunged it into his right eye.

The veil lifted off of her mind and everything became clear again. There was a sizzle as the chopstick, freshly sharpened and consecrated with magic and holy water earlier that week, burned away at the vampire's eye. The sizzle was drowned out by a howl that had never come from any human throat.

The chopstick was a good three inches deep in the bleeding, gaping wound and when the vampire tried to pull it out the hand sizzled and a thin waft of smoke rose from the palm.

With a snarl of anger she grabbed the other stick, slapped its flailing arms away and plunged it deep into where its heart should be. There was a louder sizzle this time and the twitching stopped, the thing falling to the ground.

Her body trembled from the rush of adrenaline but she only had a second to take a deep breath before she heard the deadbolt in the door slide back. She kicked off her heels, grabbed her purse, and raced towards it. It began to open just as she got to it, and with a leap she kicked at it as hard as she could. There was a satisfying crunch as the door hit something hard and human. She threw the door open and found Carlos standing stunned in the middle of the hallway, one hand clutched at his bloody nose and the other limply held his pistol.

When he saw her he wiped the blood from his lips and raised the pistol at her. She ducked in close, moving past the pistol and slamming the knife-edged space between her thumb and fingers right into his neck above the "r" and "l" of his necklace. With her other hand she grabbed his gun hand and slammed it into the wall, forcing him to drop the weapon. He was gagging weakly, hand to his damaged throat and she helped him to the ground with a knee to the groin and a headbutt to his broken nose.

As he writhed on the ground in pain, Lexie picked up his pistol, checked it, and reached into her purse for her phone.

"Henry?"

"Is it going bad?"

"That's an understatement. They tried to feed me to their bloodsucking boss, but I think I put him down. I'm going to try to get Marcia and head out the back. Meet me there, okay?"

"Wait, Lex--"

She ended the call before he could argue and set off down the hallway.

Henry jammed the phone back into his coat pocket, swearing under his breath. As soon as he'd gotten her text he'd started the car and headed around the building towards where the non-dance-club patrons entered. He'd parked closer to the alleyway leading to the back door than he would've liked, but he'd been afraid he'd miss them if they were in a hurry.

If Lexie could find Marcia at all.

If the two of them could even make it past armed guards. Not to mention the monster controlling them. Assuming there was only one.

Even if she was right and she had disposed of the vampire that was no guarantee she was going to make it out okay.

"Damn it. God damn it." He closed his eyes, tried to remember all the promises he'd made to stay safe and not take unnecessary risks, but all he could see was Mike Morrison wringing his hands with worry and Lexie's overconfident grin. He opened his eyes with a sigh and got out of the car.

The alley was dimly lit and thankfully there wasn't anyone else waiting to see if they could get in. The muscular, well-dressed black kid standing by the door watched with his head cocked and arms across his chest as Henry approached. As he walked towards him Henry glanced up and saw a camera above the door. He took a breath and focused his energy on it, expending just enough to make whoever was watching decide there was something more interesting to watch someplace else. It wasn't simple magic but easy enough for him to do while concentrating on the task at hand.

"What's up?" the kid at the door nodded at him.

"I was told this was a good place to get some action," Henry said, slurring his speech a little.

"That so. By who?"

"Hold on, hold on. Got his name right here." Henry fished around in his coat pocket and pulled out a large silver coin. The kid's brow furrowed in confusion as the coin reflected the light above the door. Henry rolled it over his knuckles as he stepped closer, the kid so entranced by the light flashing off the coin that he didn't even notice Henry's two fingers touching his forehead and the low muttering that accompanied it. After a couple of seconds the kid's eyes rolled back in his head and he slumped to the ground fast asleep.

Henry patted the kid down until he found his pistol. He slid out the clip and tossed it into the trash, followed by the round he ejected from the chamber. Henry reached back into his pocket, pulled out his lock gun, and went to work on the door. It was a little slower than magic but he didn't want to exhaust himself if Lex had more supernatural company.

Lex stopped at each doorway and listened for occupants. The first one she heard people inside of she shouldered open only to find a skinny, strung-out girl dressed like a cheerleader riding a balding, middle-aged man, both caught between ecstasy and embarrassed confusion.

"What the hell?" the girl mumbled. As soon as Lex realized she wasn't Marcia she grabbed her by the shoulder and pulled her off of him.

"Hey, I've got--" the john said sitting up, but Lex leveled the pistol she'd taken from Carlos at him and tried not to let her gaze drift downward.

"The right to remain silent," she said, finishing his thought. "Unless you get your shit together and get out right now." He nodded and began to gather his clothes in a hurry.

"Who the fuck are you?" the girl said, trying to work through the haze of whatever she was on.

"I'm looking for Marcia," Lex said, shaking her. "Marcia! Do you know where she is?"

"I . . . I think she's down the hall. Number seven. What's going on?"

Lex grabbed the girl by the hair and forced her to look

her in the eye. "Go home, okay? That thing is gone, this place is done, and you need to go home."

"Home? Wait, he can't be gone, he--"

"He's gone. Dead. Dead-er. Now go!" Lex got up, dragged the girl to the door, and gave her a push to help her on her way.

She didn't want to think about the other girls in the other rooms she wasn't going into. She just hoped that by the time all the confusion settled whatever hold the vampire had over them would be broken and they'd leave, even though the dazed look in the cheerleader's eyes though told her that they weren't just using that thing's charms alone to keep the girls in place.

"Marcia!" Lex said, shouldering in the door with the little gold seven on it.

"Jesus Christ!" the girl inside said, springing up from her knees. Despite being barely clothed and made-up to the point of clownishness, Lex recognized her from the pictures Mike had given them.

"What the fuck is this?" the muscular wannabe gangster Marcia had been servicing snarled, getting to his feet.

"Her Dad sent me," she said, putting the pistol in his

face. "And he's pissed." He raised his hands and started to back up before he tripped over the pants around his ankles.

"My Dad . . . what the hell . . . " Marcia said, shaking her head.

"C'mon Marcia, we're going home," Lex said, taking her by the arm and pulling her towards the door.

"No! Wait!" Marcia dragged her feet and when Lexie looked back at her she could see some focus returning to the young woman's eyes. "Why would my dad want me back? He said he never wanted to see me again."

"That's not true," Lexie said, loosening her grip on Marcia's arm. "He hired us to come and find you and get you out of here."

Marcia shook her head. "But he was here. He said . . . he said he hated me. That I was a disappointment and that he never loved me."

"*I think maybe he did something to me and I just can't remember*," Mike had said.

"Marcia, that monster made your father say those things. The same way he's gotten into your head and made you do things you don't want to do. Your dad loves you more than anything and he's sorry. He just wants you to come home."

The girl closed her eyes, took a deep breath, and nodded.

"All right, let's go," Lexie said, leading her out of the room. The two barely cleared the doorway when Lexie felt a gun at her temple.

"Very touching," Tony snarled, pressing the barrel against her so hard she had to tilt her head. "You may have cost me my meal ticket, you little bitch. If that's the case I'm going to be very upset with you."

"I'm shaking," Lex said. Tony took her pistol, tucked it in his belt, and shoved her shoulder, herding the two women down the hall towards the vampire's suite. One of Tony's goons was knelt down next to the body of the undead thing, holding the chopstick Lex had plunged in its eye.

"I don't think he's breathing," the thug called down the hallway.

"How fucking stupid are you?" Tony yelled. "Take the other one out!"

The thug nodded and pulled the other one out of the thing's chest with two fingers, making a disgusted face. He dropped the two sticks to the floor and leaned in close to the body. After a moment he leaned back up and shook his head.

"God damn it," Tony said, and then the thug let out a shriek of pain. Faster than any of them could see, the vampire had sprung up and latched onto his neck. Tony stopped walking and Lexie stepped back, pushing his gun arm against the wall with one hand and swinging back with the other. She hit him twice in the mouth before grabbing and turning his wrist to make him drop his gun.

"Marcia, run!"

With a wince of pain Tony reached out to try to grab Marcia as she ran by but Lex scooped up the pistol he dropped and smashed him across the face with it, sending up a spray of blood accented by a couple of teeth. He fell against the wall, not moving.

"Hurry!" Lex yelled, running after Marcia toward the opposite end of the hall from the vampire's room.

"Girls."

Marcia's feet went into slow motion, dragging along the carpet and stopping so short that Lexie almost bowled her over. Even just the single word made Lexie's head tingle but she grabbed Marcia's arm and pulled.

"Where do you think you're going?" it echoed in Lexie's head again and Marcia began to turn to walk towards it.

Lex dug in her heels and pulled, dragging her back a step.

"She wants to take me to my Dad."

"She's a bad person, like your father is. He never loved you, not like I do. Don't you want to stay with me and love me forever?" The voice was crawling through her again. Lex could only imagine what it was doing to Marcia after weeks of listening to it.

"Yes!" the girl shrieked, pulling against Lexie's grip. Lex gritted her teeth and then swung Marcia against the wall. The impact rattled through Lex's arm and Marcia went limp. She let her slide down to the ground and turned towards the vampire, bringing the pistol to bear and squinting down the barrel.

"Well, you are a bad person aren't you?" it chuckled, walking towards her with a steady, unhurried pace.

"You're not even a person so I don't think you're in a position to judge." Her squinting and the pistol in front of her kept the vampire mostly out of sight but she could see the eye she'd stabbed had healed and there was no wound under the hole in its shirt.

"You're going to have to try harder than that," he said, tapping the stain on his chest.

Marcia moaned and shifted at Lex's feet. She was about to pull the trigger when it wagged a finger at her. "Don't." She felt her finger lock into place, immobile. The vampire smiled bright and sharp. "You're never getting out of here. Especially not with her. But you've got moxie, I'll give you that. Drop the pistol and get on your knees. Unless you want me to make her stop you."

The pistol wobbled in Lexie's grip, but she gritted her teeth and grabbed it with her other hand, mentally screaming at her finger to work. The vampire was almost ten feet away, so close that she couldn't avoid the bloodred eyes without closing hers or looking away. She knew the second she did either it'd spring on her and feast, but her only chance was that it would free her long enough to blow this thing back to hell.

"Stop!" Henry yelled running up from behind her. The vampire hissed, mouth going inhumanly wide as it bared its fangs. Henry stopped at her side and put a hand on her shoulder.

Henry yelled something vaguely Latin that made her tingle all over and there was a burst of light from something above their heads held in his other hand. The vampire shrieked like rusted metal and threw his hands up trying to shield itself from the light. She could see it clearly now, the flesh no longer smooth and black but cracked, rotten, and gray, pulled tight over a skeletal frame. With all sense of him gone from her mind she focused on the hole in his shirt and fired off four shots. The vampire stumbled backwards, the shrieking abruptly ceased. She shrugged off Henry's hand and walked over to the body, stood over it and emptied the rest of the clip into what passed for its heart.

"Please tell me that will do it," she said, stepping back and letting out a deep breath.

"It should," he said, putting the charm back into his pocket and reaching down for Marcia. "Let's get out of here before we find out if I'm wrong."

Most of the doors in the hallway had opened and the johns occupying them poked their heads out, with some of the girls that had been servicing them right behind them. All had confused looks on their faces. "All right," Lexie yelled, putting her hands on her hips. "This is the police. Everyone stay where you are."

The confused looks were replaced with panic as johns darted down the hallway for the back staircase that Henry had come up, many of them still pulling on clothes as they ran.

Some of the girls looked around and began to follow suit.

"Some things never change. C'mon, let's get her out of here." They helped Marcia to her feet.

"What happened?" she said.

"You got knocked out. But don't worry, that thing's gone now," Lexie said, letting the girl lean on her. As they walked past Tony he stirred and tried to pull himself up. Lex helped him back down with a kick across the face. She could feel Henry glower at her as they walked down the stairs.

"Is there a problem?"

"Later," he said.

By the time they reached the bottom of the stairs Marcia had fully regained consciousness. From the way her hands trembled when she let herself into the back seat of the car, Lex wondered if it was the first time she'd been fully conscious in all of the weeks she'd been gone. Henry waved for Lex to get in on the driver's side. As they sped off he took out his phone and called Mike.

"Mr. Morrison, it's Henry Churchill . . . yes, actually she's with us right now . . . No, I think you should wait until we get there, but I'm going to need you to pack a bag for the two of you . . . I'll explain when we get there . . . okay, we'll be there soon, I'll talk to you then." He flipped the phone shut and put it in his jacket pocket.

"Why does he need to pack a bag?" Marcia asked from the back seat.

"It's just a precaution," Henry said, looking out the window.

He was silent the rest of the way to Mike's apartment.

When they got there, Marcia got out of the car and stared up at the building. "Did he really not say those things?" she asked. Lexie nodded and the two headed into the building with Henry trailing behind them. Mike buzzed them in and met them on the stairs halfway up to his apartment. He stopped when he saw her and Marcia wrapped her arms around herself and looked down at the ground.

"I'm sorry, Daddy," she said in a soft voice.

"It's okay," Mike said stepping forward and wrapping his arms around her. "I'm sorry too. I missed you so much, baby. I love you."

"I love you too, Daddy."

The two held each other silently until Henry cleared his throat. "We should head inside," he said. Mike nodded and led them up to his apartment, keeping a hand on Marci as if he were afraid she'd vanish again. Three bags sat in the doorway, all packed so full they were nearly bursting.

"I wasn't sure what to take," Mike said, waving at them. "I might've over done it."

"That's okay," Henry said. "Things got a little more intense than we normally like, so it might be safer if you and Marcia went out of town for a while."

"What do you mean 'intense?'"

Henry turned to look at Lex and then back at the Morrisons. "We severely disrupted their operation at the night club. The creature that was controlling your daughter has been dealt with but his associates may still be out there. There's a chance there will be reprisals."

Mike looked from Henry to Lexie and back again. "What does that mean?"

"Blowback," Lexie muttered.

"What the fuck are you talking about?" Mike said.

"It means they may want revenge. Your daughter was with them for a long time and they know things about her. They may come looking for her, so it's best that you aren't here if they do."

"Where the fuck are we supposed to go?"

"Stay with a friend or family member. Preferably one not in the city. Give it a couple of weeks and we'll let you know if things are okay."

Mike kept looking from one to the other, the confused relief on his face giving way to anger. "What the hell did I pay you two for? So we can go into hiding for the rest of our lives?"

"It's not the rest of your lives, Mr. Morrison. It's just--" Henry started but Lexie stepped between them.

"You paid us to get your daughter back. We did. That thing that was controlling her, the one that you saw and that fucked with your head, is dead. Gone. Whoever comes after you will just be regular men that anyone, including the police, can deal with. If they even bother to track you down. Which I doubt."

"Why's that?" Mike snapped.

"There are plenty of other people for them to go after first," she said. Lexie turned on her heel and walked out.

"Give it a couple of weeks, just to be safe. I'll be in touch," Henry said, following her out.

Lexie was already in the car when Henry came down,

this time in the passenger seat. He got in, started the car, and drove them back to the office without saying anything. They parked the car at their garage and when Henry got out, still without saying anything, Lexie waited for a moment and then followed him with an exasperated sigh.

"Maybe I'm just being overly sensitive, but I think maybe you're mad or something," she called after him.

Henry stopped and turned around. "I'm not mad I'm just--"

"I swear to fuck if you say 'disappointed' I'm gonna throw one of these stupid shoes at you. I'm not one of your kids, Henry."

"I know you're not!" He clamped his mouth shut and ran a hand over the uniformly short hair on his head. "It's just that this wasn't the way to do this. We should've planned better and waited to see--"

"God only knows what would've happened to her in that time! Who knows how long some . . . thing like that even keeps its victims around for. We had to do something, and this worked."

"It worked because we got lucky. You got lucky. They might come after her and I don't know how long I can keep tabs on them. Hell, they had cameras there. They probably have pictures of you. They may even have pictures of me. They could recognize us."

Lexie waved a hand at her revealing outfit. "I don't think anyone's going to recognize me in this."

"Maybe not, but I bet the guy you kicked the crap out of will try."

"I'm not afraid of him, Henry. I don't know if you noticed but I can handle myself."

He took a deep breath. "It's not just you I have to worry about. I have a family. I do things a certain way for a reason. I made promises that this part of my life will never affect them and I have to keep that promise. No matter what."

"Even if it means letting someone else suffer?"

He paused, rubbing his head again. "That's what I thought," Lexie said. "For what it's worth, I'm sorry. I saw an opportunity and I took it and yeah, it was a little reckless."

"A little?"

"Okay, so I sort of almost got myself killed. But I did kill a vampire so I think I deserve a victory beer before we call it a night."

"Fair enough," he said.

"Great. Because I can't wait to get out of this getup." She gave him a playful slug on the arm and they headed towards the office. "And you're buying the beer."

Heart of Suffering

July

"So I think my ex-boyfriend is trying to kill me. Y'know . . . with magic."

Lexie Winston tried to keep from rolling her eyes.

"What makes you think that, Ms. Grant?" Henry Churchill asked, leaning back in his chair and steepling his fingers under his chin. Since he'd been doing this for quite a bit longer than Lexie, she trusted him to be able to separate the wackos from the folks that were actually in real danger from the supernatural. In the nine months she'd worked with him there hadn't been many cranks that had visited their offices in upper Manhattan, but just enough for them to try her patience immensely. There'd been enough mundane investigation work that she'd been trying to get a hang of and the last thing she wanted was to be distracted by random lunatics that thought their cell phone was haunted.

"This is going to sound crazy," Helen said. She sat cross-legged on the couch in their office, Lexie and Henry facing her in separate chairs across a well-worn coffee table.

"That's all we get, day in and day out around this place," Lex said, getting a sideways glare from Henry.

"Go ahead," he said.

"It was my cat, Sparks," Helen said. "I was in my apartment last week, watching some TV when I heard Sparks start whining really bad. I thought he just wanted food so I ignored him at first, but after a couple of minutes he came over, sat right in front of the couch, looked up at me and then . . . said something."

"Your cat talked?" Lex said.

"Yeah." She brushed a strand of dyed blonde hair out of her face. "Not in a meow-that-sounded-like-words way, but an honest-to-god, clear sentence in this horrible, high-pitched scratchy voice. He said 'Why did you do it, precious?' He rolled over and began to twist around, screeching and howling. I just sat there because I was so shocked, but I could tell that he was in pain. Before I could do anything he just . . ." Her hands had clenched into fists in front of her while she was talking and after she trailed off she opened them suddenly.

"He did jazz hands?" Lexie asked.

"No! He . . . exploded."

"Exploded?" Henry said.

Helen wiped her eyes and took a deep breath, nodding. "Yeah, like something tore him from the inside out. There were just pieces, everywhere. And blood. I got up screaming and ran out of the apartment. I was gone for hours and had to convince myself I'd imagined it before I could even think about coming back. Sparks' body, what was left of it, was still there but this had happened." She took her phone out of her purse and thumbed through it before handing it across the table.

Henry took it and Lexie leaned in to examine the photo on the screen. That close the differences between the two investigators were stark. She was in her late twenties, lean and muscular with pale skin and sharp-edged features, her black hair pulled tight in a long pony tail. He was in his mid-forties, short and round with chestnut brown skin and hair peppered with gray and uniformly close-cropped from his head down to his beard.

The picture was a wide shot of Helen's living room and on the floor between the TV and the sofa were the remains of Sparks the cat. Blood spattered all over the hardwood floor of the room, but in the center there was a circle nearly clear of gore and cat parts. "There's more after that one," Helen said.

Henry nodded. After a couple of seconds Lexie made a wagging motion with her finger. "You have to use your fingers. It's not magic."

"I know how to use a phone," he muttered, swiping a finger across the screen.

The next one was a close up of the clear spot on the floor. Along the edges of the circle there were symbols smeared in blood. Given the way Henry's brow creased when he saw them, she could tell he recognized them. The next picture was of the center of the circle where most of Spark's remains lay and just underneath the lower half of his body a word was unevenly scrawled in blood.

"Precious."

There were a couple of other shots of the word and some of the symbols from other angles, but the message and intent were clear. Henry handed her back her phone. "Why 'Precious?'" Lexie asked.

"It was his pet name for me. I guess it was like a Lord of the Rings thing."

"One of those, huh? Did he ever have a history of violence? Short temper, anything like that?"

"No," Helen said. "Martin was nice guy. A little over-dramatic at times but I never thought he'd be dangerous."

"If he was so sweet, why'd the two of you split up?" Lex said.

"I guess I just didn't like where it was going," Helen sighed. "We got together our last year of college and I thought it'd just be this fun and relaxing thing, but after we graduated he started talking about spending the rest of our lives together and I just didn't really want to have to deal with that. I mean, we're only 23. Who wants to plan the rest of their life already? So after going round and round with him about it I just left. Maybe it was the wrong way to go about it, but when he was at work one day I just packed up my stuff and moved in with a girlfriend of mine. That was a little over a month ago. I knew he'd take it hard but I never imagined anything like this. This is just so . . . unreal."

"That's why they call it magic," Lex said.

"I can't even believe that! I figured it had to be magic because . . . well, what the hell else would do that? But for magic to be real and Martin to have discovered it just so he could do this is just kind of mind-blowing."

"Did he ever show any interest in the occult?" Henry asked "Did you ever see him with strange books, things like that?"

"No. Just general nerd-type stuff but nothing that looked like any kind of how-to guide."

"Thankfully there aren't very many how-to guides," Henry said. "Those symbols show some relatively strong magic at work here."

"Great. What can you do to protect me if he tries something like this again?"

"There are things I can to do make sure he can't use magic like this on you, but other than that all we can do is try to track him down and convince him to stop."

"How are you going to do that?" Helen asked.

"I have several choice firearms for occasions such as

this," Lex said with a smile.

Henry cleared his throat. "Given that he didn't show any aptitude for this before you two split up, he's probably working out of some sort of text or object that he found," Henry said. "If we take that away he won't be able to use magic to threaten you."

"So what do I do in the meantime?"

"You can stay here while I go check out his place and see what I can find."

Helen looked around the small office. Just past the area they were sitting in were Lexie and Henry's desks sitting at right angles to each other with just enough room on the other side for a wide bookshelf and a file cabinet. There was another door on the same wall as the one she came in, but after craning her neck she could see it was just a supply closet.

"You want me to stay . . . here?"

"The good news is that's a fold-out couch. The bad news is that it's about as comfortable as a fold-out couch," Lexie said with a smile.

"There's no way any magic Martin has gotten his hands on can reach you here. This building has plenty of wards on it that only the most highly skilled magician can break through," Henry said.

"And if it turns out that he's highly skilled?" Helen asked.

"There's little chance of that, Ms. Grant," he said. "Even if he got his hands on a book of exceptionally powerful magic he'd be more likely to drive himself crazy than to actually be able to use it. The power to wield that kind of magic requires training and sacrifice. Not something you can do in just a month."

"It's weird to think of something like magic having so many rules," she said.

"It's a part of the universe, Ms. Grant," Henry gave a little smile. "The universe likes it when things play by the rules."

They had Helen sit in the reception area as they got ready. Henry was checking the information she'd given him about Martin on his computer while Lexie laid out what she was going to take with her when they went to pick up some of Helen's things.

"We do have other clients, you know," she said, taking a small bottle of pepper spray and a tactical baton out of her desk drawer. "Not to mention some other commitments."

"True. But this one is in danger right now and no one else can help her. Besides, this shouldn't take too long." He looked over to see her clip the baton and pepper spray to her belt. "Do you think those'll be necessary?"

"I don't know. What I do know is that someone was concerned I wasn't being cautious enough so I decided to make sure I played it safe," she said, unlocking another desk drawer and taking her pistol out. They hadn't talked much about their first major disagreement since they started working together, but the atmosphere had gone back to normal from the icy civility of the past couple weeks.

"Very funny," he said, going back to his work. "Martin hasn't updated anything on his Twitter or Facebook since a day or so after his attack on Helen's cat."

"Please tell me he didn't announce he was going to kill a cat on the internet. 'BRB exploding a cat' or some nonsense like that."

"No. Just a lot of stuff about being heartbroken and how betrayed and angry he felt. It kind of tapered off about a week before he cast the spell. His last post is 'Oh man. I think I did something really stupid. Then again maybe it'll make me feel better. Kinda doubt it.'"

"Oh man, killing a cat may not make him feel better? Things are tough all over. Speaking of, does this seem normal to you? Some guy trying to get revenge on an ex using magic? Magic that apparently is difficult to come by?"

Henry leaned back in his chair and ran a hand across the top of his head. "No. It definitely seems to be something that's becoming more and more common."

"Well," Lex said, taking the Walther out of its holster and loading it. "Worst comes to worst it'll be great for business."

Henry grabbed a cab to head to Brooklyn and check out Martin's apartment. Martin hadn't been at work since Sparks' untimely demise and his boss at the bookstore made it clear that he wouldn't be welcomed back without it being some sort of emergency. Henry doubted that heartbreak and magic use would count. Lexie and Helen headed over to the parking garage where they kept the company car and then drove into Harlem where Helen's friend she'd been staying with lived.

The apartment was a narrow, railroad-style one bedroom on the fourth floor of a walk-up and it still smelled vaguely like disinfectant. Down the hallway past the kitchen, bathroom, and bedroom there was an archway leading into the living room. Lexie watched as Helen gathered up some things from a couple of suitcases stacked next to the sofa. Looking down she could see the slightly cleaner patch of floor in front of the bookshelf where Sparks had met his end.

"I was able to get the place cleaned up before Ricki saw what happened," Helen said. "She spends a lot of time at her boyfriend's and I'm hoping the two of them move into together so I can maybe sublet this place from her."

Before Lexie could reply there was a frantic knocking at the front door. "You expecting anyone?" she asked. Helen shook her head. "Stay here," Lexie said, letting her hand rest on her holstered Walther as she walked towards the door.

"Can I help you?" she called a couple of feet from the door.

"Is Helen there? I need to speak to her," a voice yelled frantically from the other side.

"No, she's not. Who is this?"

"Please! I saw her come up here and I've been waiting for her! I need to tell her something."

Lexie looked behind her and saw Helen standing by

the entrance to the living room. Lex arched an eyebrow inquisitively and Helen nodded. "Why don't you tell me and I'll give her the message?"

"No! Please, I have to talk to her! I have to let her know that I'm sorry!"

Lexie stepped forward, taking her hand off the Walther and pulling the pepper spray from her belt clip. "Martin? I'm a friend of Helen's and she told me she wants you to leave her alone, okay? Whatever it is you've done just forget about it and go on with the rest of your life."

"I can't!" he yelled, pounding on the door again. "It's not over! I need to talk to her!"

Lexie stepped up to the door and looked through the peephole. Instead of the smiling, clean-cut and scrawny Martin Green she'd seen on Helen's phone, the young man on the other side of the door was frantic and looking like he hadn't paid any attention to his appearance in days. "Martin, she doesn't want to talk to you but she told me to tell you that it most certainly is over. If I have to open this door it'll be to explain it you again after I've given you a face full of pepper spray. Are we clear?"

Martin banged his forehead against the door, giving

Lexie a close-up look at his matted hair. "You don't understand," he mumbled. "I have to talk to her. It's the only way I can end this."

"For fuck's sake," Helen said. She walked up to Lexie without her noticing and before she could send her back to the living room Helen pounded on the door. "Martin!" she hollered through the door. "It's over, you little weirdo! I don't know how you killed my cat, but that was sick! You know how much I loved him and now I never want to see you again, okay? Just fuck off and leave me alone!"

At the sound of her voice Lexie could see Martin snap his head up at attention. "Helen!" he started shouting before she was even finished. "You have to listen to me! I'm sorry and you have to forgi--" his plea stopped as he cried out and then banged his head against the door hard enough to make it rattle in its frame. Helen jumped back with a gasp and Lexie moved the girl behind her.

"Martin," Lexie said. "I need you to calm down, okay?"

Loud snarls and grunts echoed from the other side of the door as he pounded on it again. His yelling had devolved into animalistic howls of pain and exertion.

"Martin! Knock it off, okay?" Helen yelled, anger

fading from her voice and being replaced with worry.

"Go wait in the living room," Lexie said, giving her a nudge back down the hall. Helen took a few steps back and then stopped when Martin started pounding on the door again.

"Go!" Lexie yelled. Lex walked up to the door as she heard Helen quickly walk down the hall. Martin's pounding was beginning to taper off and the yells were trailing off into low painful moans. "Martin," Lexie called through the door. "You need help. If you like I can call someone for you, but if you keep pounding on this door I'm going to douse you with so much pepper spray you're going to think you were skull-fucked by a habañero. Clear?"

When there was no answer she put an eye to the peephole to see what he was doing. The hallway looked clear and she wondered if he'd wandered off, but then he sprung up from below, face pressed against the door. For a second he looked normal, but his pupils suddenly grew, filling his entire eye before the black turned to an angry, glaring red. The stubble on his face began to spread up his cheeks, thickening and darkening as cheekbones began to shift and expand with a series of cracks that echoed through the door. Martin opened his mouth to let out another yell and she could see his teeth being pushed aside as a row of dirty yellow fangs burst through his gums.

"Ahh shit," Lexie said, stepping back from the door. She dropped the pepper spray and drew the Walther from its holster. The roar that came from the other side of the door was anything but human.

"What the fuck is that?" Helen said, sticking her head into the hallway.

"Is there a porch or fire escape or something back there?" Lexie said, aiming the gun at the door as she backed towards the living room.

"There's a deck that leads--" she was cut off by a blow to the door that set cracks through it.

"Go! Now! Get to the car!"

"But what about--" there was another blow, this time sending parts of door flying into the hallway as a quartet of black claws broke through. Lexie heard Helen scream and take off as she stepped back even farther. The claws tore free, leaving a hole in the door, and then they and the giant, black-fur-covered arm they were attached to cleaved the door in half. The thing that had been Martin Green was massive, so big it barely fit through the doorway. The black and red eyes were wide, set dccp in its flat, leathery, ape-like face. It opened its mouth to roar at her, revealing more of the jagged teeth that were still bloodstained and moist from their eruption from Martin's jaw. On top of his head were a set of curved horns that gouged the top of the doorframe as it pushed its way into the apartment. It was covered head-to-toe in thick, black fur and wore the tattered remnants of Martin's clothes.

Lexie backed up into the living room as the thing shambled forward, keeping herself in the doorway as it approached. When it was fully in the hallway and she was confident she could hit it center mass and not send any stray rounds into the apartment across the hall, she fired. The thing took four hollow-point rounds to the chest and paused only to roar and to smash an arm into the wall in frustration.

"Fucking wonderful," Lexie muttered, holstering the pistol. She grabbed the bookshelf on the wall perpendicular to the hallway and pulled it down. It fell diagonally across the doorway and wedged itself into the wall. The thing roared in anger and she turned and ran, feeling its massive footfalls rattle along the floor as it followed after her. There was a small mud room that led to the back deck and stairs leading down into the alley below. She made it to the door before there was a crash of breaking wood and a spray of books sailed into her back and over her head. Lexie turned the lock on the door to the deck and pulled it closed behind her. The deck was small and had a couple of chairs so Lexie grabbed one and wedged it as best she could under the doorknob.

She jumped down the stairs to the deck of the apartment below Helen's and nearly landed on top of her. "What is it?" Helen yelled, stumbling backwards.

"Angry! Now go! Go!"

Helen scampered down the next flight of stairs and above them they could hear the thing that used to be Martin pounding its way through the door. They made it down to the alley that ran behind the apartment just in time to see a shower of wood and debris fall to the ground from above as the thing made its way onto the deck with an angry howl.

Helen shrieked and started to take, off but Lexie grabbed her and pulled her in the other direction towards the street where they parked. They could hear the creaks and groans of the deck and stairs as the thing made its way after them. Lexie looked over her shoulder as it made it to the second floor and when it saw them it gave another bellow, plowed right through the wooden deck railing, and jumped down to pursue them, running along on all fours like some kind of demonic gorilla.

She turned back and ran faster, pulling Helen along with her as they darted across the street towards the car. Lexie opened the door and dove in, reaching across to open the passengers side before Helen yanked the handle off with her frantic pulling. Lex had the car started before Helen got the door all the way closed and they shot out onto the street with a squeal of tires. Lexie caught a flash in the mirror of the black-furred thing leaping across the street at them and landing in the spot where the car used to be. There was another howl of rage that rattled the car windows and in the rear view mirror she could see the thing running after them in a murderous, primate shamble.

"Hold on," Lexie said, stomping down on the gas as they sped towards the next street. At the corner she twisted the wheel and the car made the turn with groans of protest. The black blur was in the rear view again and the car shook and fishtailed into the other lane as the beast hit the back corner of the car. A car in the other lane blared its horn and swerved out of their way and then back again, skidding to a stop across both lanes in front of their simian pursuer. It jumped up onto the roof of the other car and howled up into the air as Lexie and Helen sped off. Watching the thing pound its chest in frustration Lexie thought she'd have to turn around and save the occupants of the car it was having a tantrum on, but the thing turned and leaped away back towards Helen's apartment.

"Jesus Christ. Jesus Christ," Helen mumbled. "That thing . . . what the fuck was that thing?"

"Big. Angry. Like I said." Lex said, turning on to another street and then another, still checking the rear view mirror.

"No, seriously," Helen said, "What happened to Martin? Did that thing get him?"

"Not . . . exactly."

"What do you mean? Oh my god, was that Martin? Did he turn himself into that?"

"Looks like it."

"Holy shit. Why? How?"

"Excellent questions," she said, digging her phone out of her pocket now that she was reasonably sure that they weren't being followed. She dialed Henry's phone and he picked up on the second ring.

"We have a problem," she said, explaining the big,

horned, furry Martin.

"That's not good."

"No kidding. Where are you?"

"On the Triborough bridge. I should be at his apartment soon and hopefully he left some things there so I can figure out what he's done to himself."

"Fingers crossed. I'm going to drive around for a bit and make sure we lost him. Should I still go back to the office?"

"Best bet. If I can't find anything at his place, I'll come back and we'll explore some other options."

"Hopefully those options will involve a rocket launcher."

Martin's apartment was in a small complex just off Astoria Boulevard. There wasn't anyone around and in the fading afternoon light Henry was able to slip around back and locate the apartment's back door. He listened to make sure there wasn't anyone or anything in there before he jimmied the lock and made his way inside.

The back door led into the kitchen of the small, one bedroom apartment. Just beyond the kitchen was a small living room decorated with movie posters. A small couch sat in front of a TV flanked by bookshelves on the far wall. Behind the couch and against the wall was a small desk with a computer. In the living room he could smell something foul coming from deeper in the apartment. It wasn't strong, but it was a mix of rotting meat and sulfur that was all too familiar to him.

He glanced at the stacks of papers and magazines as he walked back towards the bedroom. He put his ear to the door and, after he was sure the room was empty, he opened it. The blood and sulfur smell breezed over him and he turned to take in a breath of fresh air.

The room was small and cramped, a twin bed pushed against the far wall and a bookshelf made with milk-crates and wooden planks on the other. Clothes were strewn around the room in piles of various sizes and odors. The center of the room was clear of mess and a five foot square had been cut in the thin, cheap carpeting. On the square of concrete and drawn in the familiar dark brown of dried blood was a circle, complete with runes, symbols, and a pentagram. At the points of the pentagram sat candles, all burned down to the floor. Next to the door was a book open to a page that had an image of the circle that had been drawn on the floor.

Henry walked in a slow circuit around the circle and when he was convinced every line was solid and the symbols were exactly what he initially thought they were, he turned his attention to the book. It was a small, thin leather-bound hardcover that had seen better days. He leafed through it, noting that the type was old and there were handwritten notes in places. Much of the book had to do with demonic summoning rituals. While he wasn't familiar with this exact volume, he could see the resemblance to another book he'd come across a couple of months ago.

This opened up a whole other set of problems, but he knew he needed to focus on the matter at hand.

Henry headed back into the living room, taking off his suit jacket and opening his phone. As he waited for Lex to pick up, he rolled his sleeves up to his elbows.

"Any luck?," she said when she answered.

"A little. Martin definitely found a way to get his hands on some pretty advanced magic, mostly of the demon-summoning kind."

"Everyone needs a hobby, I guess."

"Clearly Martin bit off a little more than he could chew. I'm not sure what he was originally after, but this is pretty advanced stuff for someone who didn't know what he was getting himself into. There's a very good chance that whatever he summoned and tried to bargain with turned the tables on him."

"Hence his morphing into the demonic ape-boy."

"Exactly. There's a chance I can reach whatever it is he summoned and get it to release him from its grasp, but it's going to take a while."

"What should I do if Martin decides to pay us a visit? I put four hollow point rounds in him and he just shrugged them off."

"Hopefully he won't, but if he does the enchantments on the office and the building should be able to keep him out."

"Should? That's not going to reassure our client who has been understandably . . . tense since we got back here."

"I can imagine. Everything else I can think of could possibly hurt Martin as well and I'm not ready to give up on him just yet."

"Are we that concerned with the well-being of some guy who can't take no for an answer?"

"He's in over his head and needs our help as much as she does. Besides, haven't you ever had your heart broken and done something stupid?"

"Sure," Lexie said. "And then I graduated high school."

"Either way I'll be working on my end to stop him. If you have to defend yourself there's some consecrated buckshot for the shotgun in the weapons locker. Hopefully it won't come to that."

"Ever the optimist. Keep me posted," she said before hanging up.

Henry put his phone and coat on the couch in the living room, along with his keys and wallet from his pockets. The only things he took back to the bedroom were a small pocket knife and lighter. He made another orbit around the summoning circle just to be sure and when he was satisfied he opened the knife and drew the blade across his palm. Blood welled up in the cut as he tucked the knife away. Dipping the fingers of his other hand in the blood, he knelt down and began to add more runes and markings to the pentagram. When he was done he picked up what smelled like the cleanest shirt in the piles of discarded laundry and wrapped it around his bleeding hand. He lit the remains of the candles and then sat cross-legged in front of the pentagram, closed his eyes, and began to chant.

It had been about an hour since Henry had called and

Lexie was pretty sure that if he didn't call back soon she was going to go out and hunt Martin the Man-Ape down herself. After the initial shock of being chased wore off, Helen became increasingly irritated at the idea of being cooped up in the small office until something was done about it.

"This blows. You can't just keep me prisoner, y'know? I am paying you. Well, my dad is paying you but you know what I mean. Can't you do something about this?"

Lexie took a deep breath and tried to concentrate on the crossword puzzle she was doing.

"Sure. If you'd like we can swing by your old place again and see if Martin's made a nest out of your clothes. That could be an exciting change."

Helen let out an irritated sigh and narrowed her eyes. Lexie tried to remember that the young woman was under a lot of stress and that she needed someplace to focus her anger and fear. She also tried to remember that hitting clients probably wasn't a good way to get them to pay. Helen got off the sofa and began another walk around the office. She started by the windows, which just looked out on the alley running behind the building, and then moved on to the bookshelves by Henry's desk and stared at the strange titles. She paused to glare at the shotgun leaned up against the wall by the door and then walked out to the reception area to lean her head against the glass door to the hallway like a forlorn zoo animal.

"How come your name isn't on the door?" Helen called back into the office.

"What do you mean?," Lexie said, getting up and joining her in the smaller reception room.

Without turning around Helen tapped on the lettering facing the hallway which read:

Churchill

Private Detectives

Just above the Churchill you could see a faded, almost scraped off ampersand. "You should've seen how long it took Henry to take the other name off. I doubt he's in a hurry to add mine anyway."

"Why's that?"

Lexie stopped herself from saying, "Because I killed his old partner," and simply shrugged.

"Does it bother you?" Helen said, turning around to face her and leaning on the door.

Lex shook her head with a small smile. "Not really. Besides, my last name would look kind of goofy on there anyway."

"Really? What is it?"

"Winston."

Helen smiled for the first time that Lexie could remember. "Wow, that'd be hilarious. You guys should get a bulldog or something as a mascot."

Lex shook her head. "Can't. I'm allergic to picking up something else's shit."

Helen laughed, but just as Lexie thought the good mood would hang around for a while it faded into an exhausted sigh and she slumped back against the door. "How much longer do you think he's going to be?"

Lexie shrugged. "No idea. He's good at this stuff so I'm sure it won't be too much longer."

Helen let out a groan and headed back into the office, brushing past Lexie. "God I hope not. I'm really not looking forward to sleeping on the couch." Helen dug through her purse until she found her pack of cigarettes and walked over to the window with it. Then she opened it and saw there was only one left. "Fucking hell. Now this?" she showed the lone, soon-to-be-smoked cigarette.

"You're lucky I'm letting you smoke in here at all," Lexie said. "With the window open you're letting out all the air-conditioning."

"You could let me go outside and it wouldn't be a problem."

"Until Martin shows up to do . . . whatever it is an angry demon ape does to an ex-girlfriend."

Helen gave that sigh again, as if having her life saved was the biggest inconvenience she'd ever had to endure. "You could at least let me go to that store downstairs and get another pack."

"Don't worry about it," Lex said, turning around and heading out the door. "I'll get them for you. I've been dying for some non-temperature-controlled air anyway." She almost kept from slamming the door behind her as she headed out into the hallway. Their office was on the second floor of a small building and across the hall from them and facing the street was an accountant's office. At one end of the hall was the bathroom the two offices shared and at the other was the stairway leading down to the street and the convenience store in the first floor storefront.

Lex headed down, taking the stairs two at a time as she tried to burn off as much frustration and irritation as she could. The young man at the market smiled when Lexie came in, but didn't try any of his pointless flirting as she bought a pack of cigarettes for Helen and an iced tea for herself. As she stepped outside Lexie realized that she could still feel herself flush with irritation. She stopped on the sidewalk and took a long drink of her tea as she tried to keep herself calm.

She looked up, closed her eyes, and took a deep breath. She opened her eyes just in time to see a large black shape leap from the taller building next door down to the roof of their office building.

"Ah, fuck!" she shouted, dropping her tea and running for the door as she pulled out her keys. She flung it open and darted up the stairs. "Helen!" she yelled as she rounded the corner at the top and darted down the hall. "Helen!" Lexie practically plowed through the door and into the reception area.

"What?" Helen said, still wearing the same look of irritated boredom. "I'm keeping it outside!" Helen wagged the arm that was holding her cigarette and dangling out of the second floor window. Before Lexie could say anything, the black-furred shape that she'd seen reached down from the outside of the building, grabbed Helen's hand, and yanked her out the window.

Lexie was almost able to grab Helen's ankle before she was completely pulled outside screaming in pain and surprise. Lexie looked out the window and could see Martin the demonic Man-Ape clinging to the side of the building with one hand and both feet while holding the kicking and screaming Helen at arm's length. With a howl of triumph he pulled himself up the side of the building and onto the roof, dragging Helen with him.

Lexie ran back through the office, grabbing the shotgun and heading for the stairs, leaving a wake of profanity trailing behind her.

Even with his eyes closed Henry could sense the change in the room. The air felt charged with static electricity and smelled of burning metal. Something from the other side was crossing over. He opened his eyes and could see the candles burning higher now, the sole illumination as the sun had just set outside. The smoke from the nearly foot-tall flames was gathering at the ceiling, coiling along the edges of the summoning circle as if it was trying to find a way out.

Henry knew it wouldn't find one.

The smoke began to drift down towards the ground, curling into a pile and becoming thicker and darker the closer it got to the ground. It thickened and solidified, taking the form of a naked woman sitting in the fetal position. Her skin began to lighten until it became a nearly translucent white, but her hair remained coal black and floating on a nonexistent breeze. She slowly opened her arms and raised her head, taking in the whole room before settling her gaze on Henry. She stretched with a smile and began to crawl towards Henry on all fours, a wry smile on her face. Her hair drifted around her as she crawled, keeping her mostly covered while showing just enough to try to tantalize.

"You summoned me," she said, her voice echoing and deep enough that Henry could feel it inside his body. She came right to the edge of the circle and stretched her arms wide in the air as she remained on her knees, rolling her head around and making her hair drift and sweep over her body, revealing a hint of her nakedness.

"I am here to do your bidding," she said, bowing her head and sweeping her arms towards him, palms up.

"I doubt that," Henry said.

"You summoned me, didn't you? I am here at your bidding for whatever you desire."

"Fine," Henry said. "I want you to release your hold over the mortal Martin Allen Green. He summoned you before from this room."

The smile dropped from her face and the green of her eyes darkened. As he stared at her, Henry could see that under her pale white skin ripples pressed into her flesh from inside her body, swirling like the smoke that was her hair.

"Why do you want this?" She pouted, tilting her head to the side and letting her hair float in front of her. "That is a different transaction. That has no bearing on us."

"It has as much bearing as I want it to. Release your hold over him. Undo whatever power you've granted him. Whatever bargain you've made with him is finished."

Her pouting lips turned in a sneer. She considered Henry for a moment and then threw her head back in a terrible approximation of a laugh. "You have no dominion over me. You offer me no bargain. You have no power here."

Henry took a deep breath. "I can offer you your freedom."

The demon's laugh stopped and she looked back at

him with contempt. "Do not overstep, mortal. This circle summons, but does not bind. You would best tread carefully."

"As should you."

The demon hissed and leaped towards him, black fingernails extended and crashing into the invisible wall of circle. It clawed and scratched at the air only inches from Henry's face, but he didn't blink.

After an exasperated sigh Henry closed his eyes and began a barely audible chant. The demon's eyes grew wide and it howled in pain, throwing itself at the boundary of the circle. Henry kept the chant going for a full five minutes before he stopped and opened his eyes. There were beads of sweat on his forehead and he loosened his collar.

"Do you doubt me now?" he said once he caught his breath.

The demon looked up at him from the floor, green eyes still blazing bright through strands of hair that were once wispy and ethereal but now matted to its form and lying flat on the ground. "You do have power. Blood sacrifice power. How many have you killed for this, mortal? How much human blood stains your hands so that you can possess such strength."

"Too much," he said. "Now release your hold on

Martin Allen Green."

The thing chuckled. "The young lover. The heartbroken mortal who wanted revenge at first, but when he saw what that would entail he became weak and begged. Begged to end the vengeance he asked for."

"What did he ask for?"

The demon sneered. "He wanted to be strong. He wanted her to hurt and to feel the pain that she had caused him."

Henry sighed. Demons were skilled at twisting the words and desires of those that summoned them. Martin almost certainly used those exact words and the demon no doubt used them as an excuse to curse Martin into whatever he had become.

"Undo it," Henry said. "You've played your game and it's over now."

The demon shook its head with a wide, evil grin. "Not over. Never over. When he begged for it to be over, to take back what he'd asked for, I told him that he must go to her and tell her of the danger waiting for her and then they both would be free. Stupid, stupid mortal."

"You wanted him to kill her, didn't you?"

The demon hissed. "He will turn into what he wanted. Something strong, something that will cause great pain. When he sees her he will kill her, damn his soul, and then he will be ours. Ours for eternity."

"No. Release him. Break your hold and I will set you free. That is the bargain I offer you. Refuse and you will suffer."

The demon thrashed and threw itself at the boundary of the circle once more, hissing and clawing against it. After a few moments its tantrum stopped and it stared at him as it leaned against the invisible boundary.

"You may have power but you're afraid to use it, aren't you? You paid too much for it and now you hold yourself back for fear of being reminded of it. Of slipping into darkness even though you know when your end comes you are damned."

Henry nodded. "That may be so. What I will tell you is that when your end comes you'll be trapped here on this plane and you'll vanish from existence. But before that happens you'll suffer unspeakably at my hands, even if it sends me to an eternity of torment at the hands of those like you. There is only one way back for you now and it's by releasing Martin Allen Green. Think of all the blood you can sense on my hands and know that most of it is from those I held dearest to me. Do you think I'd hesitate to add some from a pitiful creature like yourself? Try me, test me, and you will know my wrath."

The demon cocked its head to the side and sneered.

"Fine," Henry said. "Welcome to hell."

He closed his eyes and began to chant again as the thing in the circle screamed in pain.

Lexie raced down the hall towards the stairwell with the shotgun in hand. She'd loaded it with the consecrated buckshot that Henry had told her about. She hoped that it'd be sufficient to at least give that thing pause long enough for Helen to escape. There was a utility closet by the top of the stairs and Lexie flung open the door and kicked at the assorted mops and brooms as she made her way to the small ladder that led up to the roof. She hurried up it as best she could with the shotgun under her arm, but when she got to the top she could see that the trapdoor at the top was padlocked.

"Oh give me a break," she muttered. Keeping hold of the ladder with the arm the shotgun was tucked under, she pounded up on the small door with her free hand, putting as much of her weight into each blow as she could. After about seven strikes she could hear the wood around the clasp of the lock begin to crack. She took another step up the ladder and pressed her shoulder into it as hard as she could. With her head tilted uncomfortably, she pushed with her legs until she could hear the screws pulling from the wood. She backed down the ladder and pounded at it again. It took three tries and cost her all the feeling in her hand, but it flung open and she was able to pull herself up onto the roof.

At the other end of the roof Helen sat whimpering, holding her knees to her chest as Martin circled around her in the same knuckle-dragging gait that he pursued them with earlier. Lexie checked the shotgun and advanced, trying not to make a sound. Martin's attention was focused entirely on his captive as he circled her, shaking his head and growling. He stopped and looked down at Helen, red eyes glaring and giant fangs bared. After a moment he pounded his hands on his chest and clawed at the horns on his head and howled at the sky before resuming his orbit of Helen.

Helen looked over at Lexie and opened her mouth to shout but Lexie shook her head. Martin was circling with his back to Lexie but stopped, sniffing at the air with confusion. When he looked over his shoulder and saw Lexie he bared his teeth and growled. She raised the shotgun and Martin snarled, scurrying forward and putting himself between Lexie and Helen.

Lex stopped walking forward and Martin lowered himself closer to the ground, snarling and digging up pieces of tar with his claws. Lex took a few steps to the side to put Helen back in view, but Martin sidestepped as well, giving a series of angry barks.

"Martin," she said after a deep sigh. "I really, really don't want to shoot you if you're in there somewhere. Even though you were dumb enough to get yourself turned into a demon monkey."

Martin let out a roar.

"Or gorilla. Whichever. But here's the thing: if it's a choice between shooting you and saving her, I'll drop you in a heartbeat. This is New York City, pal. We've got a proud history of dropping apes off buildings."

Martin growled and dug his front and back claws into the roof even further.

"Don't do it, Martin. I'm serious. I want to help but I will defend myself. And her. Just back up."

Another roar. Lexie slid the stock forward, loading a shell in the chamber.

"Don't," she said right before he charged her.

Henry opened his eyes. Sweat stung them and he could taste blood in his mouth. He wasn't sure how long he'd been chanting, probably about an hour but it felt like four or five. It felt as if a lead weight was pressing into his chest and he'd lost feeling in his legs. The only thing that gave him satisfaction was that the captive demon was far worse off.

It curled on the floor, pale white skin now cracked, broken, and leaking a black, viscous ooze that the thing had smeared on the ground as it writhed in pain. Small piles of hair that it had yanked out of its head in its thrashing surrounded it. It looked up at Henry, its green eyes now dull and leaking tears of the black liquid as well. It snarled at Henry and he knew that even as it had felt to him like more time than had actually passed, for the imprisoned demon it must have seemed much longer. Perhaps even years.

Trapped on this plane time moved differently for them, and in the confines of the circle it was as helpless as a pinned insect. Henry was almost ashamed at the pleasure he felt in its torment.

"Will you agree to my bargain? Your return to your

realm in exchange for Martin Allen Green's release from your pact?"

"Never," it hissed. "You are weak. This magic will burn through you and then we will feast upon your soul. You will suffer for this."

"Fine," Henry said. He leaned forward, wincing as blood flowed back into his legs. He untied the shirt from the cut on his palm. The wound still seeped blood but he had to tug it free from the parts that had managed to scab over. He leaned forward and waited for blood to well in his palm before beginning to mark more symbols on his side of the circle.

"I will bind you to me, so that when I die from this you will endure the same torments I do. My damnation will be yours as well."

The demon shrieked and clawed at the invisible barrier dividing them. "Never! You wouldn't dare!"

Henry turned and spat a mixture of spit and blood before looking up at it, the thing now less than an inch from his face.

"Fucking try me."

He looked back down and began to scrawl again.

"No! We accept! We accept your terms!"

Henry stopped and looked up at it. Its eyes were wide with sheer terror.

"Do it," he said.

"We release the Martin Allen Green from his contract. He is free from our hold forevermore."

Henry nodded, feeling the magic ripple outwards from the circle. He leaned down and kept writing.

"You swore! You swore!" the thing screamed at him.

"You're a demon," Henry said, changing the symbols. "Why should I keep my word to you?"

Before it could do anything, he finished the last symbol and chanted again, this time only a few short lines. There was a crackling hiss from inside the circle and the demon's skin began to bubble and dissolve, congealing into a black mess before it burst into flame and left no trace it ever existed.

With a groan Henry straightened himself out, giving a yelp of pain as he flexed his bad knee. After a few seconds with his eyes closed and drawing deep, labored breaths he turned and spat up more blood on the carpet. He dragged himself to his feet and walked into the living room.

Hopefully Lexie was having a better evening than he was.

The shotgun went off with a roar, but the buckshot sailed over Martin's head. Just before she pulled the trigger Lexie could see him changing as he charged for her and she managed to pull the gun up.

Martin's demonic and ape-like features melted away and he tumbled forward, naked, and skidded to a halt at Lexie's feet.

"Ow," he said, rolling over.

"Yeah, that might leave a mark," she said, looking at the scrapes all over Martin's legs and torso and taking in more of him than she'd ever wanted to see.

"What happened?" he said, shaking his head. "Why am I naked . . . on someone's roof?"

"I wouldn't worry about it too much," Lexie said, lowering the shotgun.

"Holy shit," he muttered, wincing and looking up at her. "You've got a shotgun."

"Yup. Here's a closer look," Lexie said and then cracked him across the head with the butt of it.

"Oh my god!" Helen yelled, running over. "Is he . . ?"

"Just unconscious," Lexie said. "Now if you excuse me,

I may need to change my pants after that one." She sat down on the roof, laying the shotgun next to her. Before she could lie down her phone vibrated in her pocket. She took it out with a sigh. When she saw it was Henry she accepted the call and said, "Let me guess: you fixed it."

"Was it that obvious?"

"Well, I almost shot a guy in the face so yeah. A little obvious. Don't cut it so close next time."

He chuckled and then let loose a series of wet, painful-sounding coughs. "You all right?" she asked.

"Just fine. Just the aftereffects of a demonic banishment."

"Swell," she said, lying down. The roof still held some of the burning heat of the day and she could feel it ease the tension in her body. She held the phone up for Helen and closed her eyes. "Talk to Henry. Tell him we're on the roof. And to bring that guy some pants."

Helen left before Martin woke up and Martin woke up before Henry made it back from Brooklyn with a change of clothes for him.

"Did you knock me out?" Martin asked after covering

himself with a blanket Lexie dug out of the storage closet. They'd come down off the roof, Lexie insisting he go first down the ladder so that nothing dangled above her as she climbed.

"Yes," she said, "but in my defense you turned into a demon monkey once already today. I didn't know if you were going to have a repeat performance."

Martin put a hand to the temple Lexie had hit and winced. "Fuck. That was all real, wasn't it?"

"Yup. Good job there, sport. You almost managed to turn breaking up into a homicidal safari."

"I didn't mean to. It just got out of hand."

"That's an Olympic-level understatement."

"I should call her and--"

"I'm going to attribute that to the blow to the head," Lexie interjected. "She told me to tell you to never call her ever again. Plus she said she blocked you on Facebook, Twitter, and Tumblerer. She may have made that last one up. She did seem a little less upset when I told her that you said you'd pay our bill."

"I did what? I don't think I did that."

"Yeah, you did. Remember, I've still got that shotgun, Marty."

"You make a very convincing argument."

"That I do. Let me get you her bill. Not only do we take Visa, MasterCard, and Discover, but we also offer an installment plan."

Henry arrived with clothes for Martin who dressed before they sent him home in a cab. Lexie told him they'd add it to his bill. When the two made it back upstairs and were reclined in their chairs she finally said, "You kind of look like shit."

"Thanks."

"I mean it. Are you sure you're going to be okay?"

"Nothing a good night's rest can't fix."

Lexie wanted to pry further because he looked anything but fine. It was almost as if he'd aged noticeably since he left. "I hope so because you look like you've been dragged behind a bus."

"Fair enough," Henry said. "By the way, we have this to thank for today's troubles." He reached into the bag he'd brought Martin's clothes in and set the book of demonic summoning on his desk.

"No shit," Lexie said, sitting up to take a closer look at

it. "Am I nuts or does that look familiar?"

"It looks very familiar," Henry said. "In fact, I'm almost sure it comes from the same library as the book that Mimi Chalmers had."

"This isn't good, is it?"

"Not in the slightest."

"Did Martin say where he got it?"

"I haven't asked yet," Henry said. "I'm going to give him some time to reflect on the day's events and then see what he has to say for himself."

Lexie nodded and then put her head down on her desk. "Sounds like a plan. Do me one favor?"

"Shoot."

"Bring him a bunch of bananas when you go."

An Equal Sharing

of Miseries

April

"ICE! This is a raid," Walters yelled as the door flew open.

The Chinese men in the kitchen stared at her blankly until they noticed the badge on her uniform and the swarm of uniformed immigration officials following behind her. They put up their hands, arguing in Mandarin as she moved past them. While she and the rest of her team cleared the kitchen and dining room of the restaurant, others were making their way up stairs to the offices and makeshift apartments to round up the inhabitants and check for IDs and work permits as they sorted out the illegals.

As they moved through the building, Bonnie could see that their surveillance over the past month had been right on the money. On the second floor there was an obviously unlicensed clinic and almost every other level of the building had some sort of illegal gambling. Many of the men shouted in annoyance as they moved through, and a few tried to pick their money up off the table before the other agents stood them up and began moving them downstairs.

While there were certainly going to be enough illegals to make the raid worthwhile, there wasn't much of anything along the lines of drugs or prostitution to make it a real slam dunk.

As Bonnie and the others regrouped downstairs in the restaurant's kitchen, she tried to tell herself that she shouldn't be too dismayed at the fact that they hadn't found more evidence of the kind of abuse and other heinous acts that occasionally came for her job.

"Is that everything?" Bonnie's partner, Susan York, asked.

Bonnie nodded down a small hallway past a group of dishwashers where a lone, narrow door stood. "If that's just a broom closet then yeah, we're good."

Susan nodded and the two headed for it, Bonnie putting an ear to it as she knocked. "ICE! Show yourselves!" When there was no response she signaled Susan and stepped back as she pulled the door open, revealing a stairway lit by a single, bare bulb and leading down to another door.

"Guys!" Susan called over her shoulder. A couple of officers came over and the quartet headed down. Bonnie repeated the knock and yell on the door at the bottom, and this time she could hear high-pitched, nervous murmurs. Bonnie nodded over her shoulder and then kicked the door in.

The small group of young Chinese girls in waitress uniforms standing just inside the doorway gave yells of surprise as the officers came in. The basement room was dimly lit by a pair of fluorescent lights and had various pallets of dry goods and cleaning supplies stacked in rows. At the far end of the room she could see a tiny beam of light from the metal doors leading to the sidewalk above.

Susan stayed with the girls, telling them in Mandarin what was going on and that they needed to come with her as

Bonnie stepped farther into the basement. "I'll check the rest of the place," Bonnie said.

"Hold on," Susan said, lining the girls up and heading them up the stairs. "I'll be right there."

As Bonnie looked around, she noticed something in the far corner of the room. As she stepped closer, she could see that where the rough stone walls met there was something stuck on the wall from the floor to the low ceiling. Bonnie moved closer until she could see it was dozens upon dozens of pieces of paper stuck to the wall, each with a set of Chinese characters on it. As she examined them, she realized it was the same characters on each piece of paper, and the only part they didn't cover was a small doorknob on the far left side.

She put a hand on the paper and felt along the edges, finding where the seam of the door and the hinges had all been papered over. As she did, a soft noise came from the other side. She put her ear to the door and strained to listen through the rustle of the paper as she moved against it.

"Hello?" she called and she could hear the noise again. Like someone moving around slowly. She tried the doorknob, but it was locked.

"I'm coming in," she yelled, taking a utility knife out of

her pocket, she stuck it into the seam of the door, and slit the paper on the top, bottom, and left side. Whoever had papered up this door had done so a while ago, perhaps weeks or more. She didn't want to think about what condition the person on the other side could be in.

"Hey!" She yelled up the stairs, hoping Susan or any of the agents could hear her. "There's someone else down here!" Once the paper was clear of the doorknob and lock mechanism, she began to pry away at it with her knife, hoping she could pop the latch. The noise on the other side of the door got louder, like something was scratching.

"Hold on, I'm coming!" Bonnie yelled, the tip of the blade began to work its way past the tip of the lock.

"What's going on?" Susan called from the other side of the basement.

"It's a door that someone covered up," Bonnie said. "I think someone's back there."

There was an excited burst of Mandarin as one of the girls that had been taken up stairs hurried down the stairs after Susan. Susan took the girl by the arm and tried to lead her back upstairs but the young woman struggled, growing more agitated.

Bonnie turned to see if Susan needed any of her help, but as she did her blade found purchase and popped the latch of the lock. The door swung open a crack and she could smell something rotten as soon as it did. When she saw the door open, the girl on the stairs started kicking and screaming. Bonnie got to her feet, and the door flung open into her as something flew out at her with a growl and chaos erupted.

August

In a situation like this, Lexie Winston wished she were armed.

She knew the time to turn back was before she'd had herself buzzed in, but she still had pangs of doubt on the way up the elevator and down the hallway to the apartment. She always felt ill prepared and uncomfortable when going into a totally unknown situation, and while she knew she wasn't in any real danger, there was something to be said about the comfort of a trusty firearm.

"Ah, fuck it," she muttered, knocking on the door a little harder than she should've.

The door opened almost immediately and Lexie was greeted with a smile by her hostess. "Lexie, come in! We're so glad you could make it!" Monica Churchill's smile was infectious, and Lexie could feel a little bit of the nervousness slip away.

"Thanks," Lexie said, stepping into the apartment. The living room was almost as large as Lexie's whole apartment and filled with just over a dozen people in several small groups, talking and drinking as music played softly in the background. Above the television on the far wall hung a colorful banner reading, "Happy Birthday Henry!"

"You look nice," Monica said, and Lexie smiled politely even though she knew that Henry's wife didn't have much basis for comparison. She had met Lexie only once since her husband's new partner moved to New York City to work with him. Monica had been cordial and friendly despite the sudden loss of Henry's old partner and the need to restructure the private investigation agency that the two men had built together for almost twenty years.

"You have a nice place," Lexie said, and now it was Monica's turn to say thanks and smile politely. After a couple of moments fidgeting, Monica motioned towards the rest of the guests and said, "Let me introduce you to everyone."

"Sure thing," Lexie said, following her hostess. Monica was attractive, looking about half of her nearly fifty years with light brown skin and shoulder-length straightened hair. Even though Henry had told Lexie the party was, "casual," Monica was in a cocktail dress that Lexie felt certain cost more than her own wardrobe put together. She could tell as she approached the small clumps of guests that this kind of casual was far beyond the t-shirt and jeans definition that she was used to.

The feeling of unease crept back as Monica introduced her to the group, mainly people from Monica's law firm and their spouses. They all smiled and nodded and didn't stare at her plain black skirt and simple blouse even though she felt like they screamed, "thrift store." She definitely would've felt better if she were armed. Or at least in uniform.

Once the initial gazing and sizing up had occurred, then came the barrage of questions. How long had she been in the city (nine months), what did she do before she moved (police officer), how did she like working with Henry (it had its moments, which drew a laugh) and then the most awkward: how did the two of them meet. She opened her mouth to answer and then paused, not knowing how much detail the group of middle-aged lawyers knew about the specialty of Lexie and Henry's private investigation firm. She glanced over at Monica, who seemed equally stymied until her face lit up with a warm smile.

"There's the birthday boy!" she said, and Lexie let out a sigh of relief. With her partner was a pale, older man with long, white hair and a thin, wispy beard.

"I thought I heard someone come in," Henry said, meeting his wife's embrace and giving her a kiss. "Lexie, I don't think you've met Donald Porter. Don, this is Lexie Winston."

"Ah yes," Don said, extending a hand for her to shake. His grip was firmer than his thin frame would've led her to believe. "I've heard a lot about you. Nice to finally put a face to the name."

"I wish I could say likewise but this guy has been a little tight-lipped when it comes to friends of his," she said.

"Well," Don said, giving Henry a playful jab at his shoulder, "when you've been in his business as long as he has, you don't end up with too many friends. Just old goats like me who help him out with some more . . . specialized items. Hell, I'm surprised he's got more than one of us in a room at the same time."

Henry gave a sigh, and Lexie saw him look over her shoulder at the small group of Monica's co-workers standing near them. Lexie turned and saw that they had turned back to their own conversation as if the other three didn't even exist. "Don provides us with our consecrated items," Henry said, looking back at Lexie and lowering his voice. She was glad she hadn't had the chance to allude to the supernatural nature of much of their casework.

"So it's Father Don, is it?" she said.

Don shrugged. "Pastor Don, actually. I retired a handful of years ago, so now it's just Don, the guy who works at the outreach center and occasionally blesses a pile of ammunition. Or chopsticks," he said with a wink.

"Well you do good work, otherwise I wouldn't be here," she said.

"Don't thank me," Don said, nodding upwards. "Thank Him."

"Yeah, I'll get right on that."

"Oh, another one," Don said with a grin. "I love it. You two see all manner of the unholy, not to mention benefit directly from the power of faith, but when it comes to God you're all 'Well, we're not really sure about that one.' Priceless."

"No," Henry said, "There are just some things that aren't exactly cut and dried. Many things are still up for debate."

"The word of Jesus Christ isn't, but then again an attitude like that keeps me in business so I'm not going to argue too hard."

"In any case," Lexie said, "it's nice to finally meet someone else in our circle of . . . special investigations."

Don smirked. "Well, good luck with that. Now if you'll excuse me, I'm going to grab some of those canapés so I don't gorge myself on cake." He walked away, nodding and smiling at Monica's friends as he passed.

"What's that supposed to mean?" she asked.

Henry took a drink and took a couple of steps farther away from the circle of civilians behind Lexie and she followed suit. "That's Don's way of saying he wishes I were a bit more open with some of the contacts that I've made over the years. He's a good friend and I trust him implicitly, but he can be a little devout for most of the folks that I end up dealing with."

"Really? A priest who can actually bless things for use in fighting evil. Yeah, who would've thought he'd be devout."

"It's not just that. Some of the folks that I've had to

deal with play for the opposing team in Don's eyes, and I'm sure he'd be more than willing to hurry them along to their final reward given half the chance. He doesn't exactly have a lot of tolerance for things he deems unholy."

"Huh. Well, maybe I should let him know I'm gay and see what kind of tolerance he has for that," she said.

"I said he's devout, not a bigot."

"There's a difference?"

Henry sighed. "Of course there's a . . . you know what? It's my birthday. I'm not going to get into this with you. You look very nice, by the way."

She chuckled. "Nice dodge. Thanks. I feel kind of ridiculous, but what the hell, right? Every once in a while I drag out the one skirt I own and make an effort. Besides, you only turn fifty once, right?"

"It's forty-six, smart mouth," he said with a poorly-hidden grin. The two had wandered over towards the makeshift bar set up across the room. Lexie poured herself a glass of wine, and the two of them watched the rest of the folks at the party. "You guys really do have a nice place," she said after a few moments of taking the place in.

"Thanks. Did you work out that thing with your

landlord?"

"Yup. He's going to let me paint, so that's cool."

He nodded and the two of them took a drink.

"So aside from Pastor Don, are you actually friends with any of these people?" she asked.

"Sure. They're mostly folks from Monica's law firm, but I've known almost all of them for years. Plenty of work functions over the years, and the firm just keeps on growing."

"But what Don was saying about people from our line of work . . . you don't really socialize with them, do you?"

Henry stared down into his scotch before finishing it. "I do when they need my help, I need theirs, or I'm just trying to keep tabs on them. Other than that there's not that much to talk about."

"Yeah. I can imagine," she said, finishing her drink and setting the glass down on the table. "Hey, where's your bathroom?"

"Down the hall," he pointed. "Last door on the left."

"Thanks," she said, already walking away and trying not to wonder which of the three categories she fell into.

As Lexie washed her hands, she tried to shake her

sudden paranoia from her mind. She and Henry had only met last November, so she shouldn't have thought it too odd that this was her first time seeing his place and only the second time that she'd met his wife. If it weren't for the death of his last partner and the fact that she'd lost her job, been ostracized from her family, and nearly arrested upstate, she never would've moved down to the city and started working with him.

She'd lost everything, and even though it was for the right reasons, it still felt pretty fucked up sometimes. Especially when she suspected that the person she'd lost it all for was still keeping her at arm's length.

"When you've been in his business as long as he has, you don't end up with too many friends," Don had said. It seemed like that was proving to be truer each day.

She left the bathroom and headed down the hallway much less enthused to be there than before and shocked that was possible. Alcohol and cake, she reminded herself. Focus on the alcohol and cake. It wasn't as motivating as she hoped.

As she passed by one of the last doors before the hallway emptied into the living room, she noticed that it was a open a little and inside were two teenagers, a boy sitting on a twin bed looking at a tablet and a girl sitting with her back to the door playing a video game where a girl in a cheerleader outfit was dismembering zombies with a chainsaw.

"Yes!" the girl said as the character on screen completed an overly complicated and suggestive series of attacks as the screen flashed in frantic appreciation. "Finally beat him!"

"Cool," the boy said, not looking up. "Now you're up to where I was a month ago."

"Ass," she said, not looking back at him.

Lexie realized just standing in the hallway watching them was more than a little creepy and started to walk away when the boy stopped her. "You're Dad's new partner, right?"

"Um, yeah," Lexie said, stopping in place. She'd known about Henry's kids but realized that aside from their names and ages she didn't know anything else. There were no pictures in the office and he never shared any, and any questions about them were casually deflected.

"I'm John," the sixteen year-old said, looking up and leaning forward with an offered hand. He was lanky with short hair and an awkward smile on his face. She stepped into the room that was probably his, given the basketball posters on the wall occasionally interrupted by ones of various supermodels.

"Lexie," she said, taking his hand.

"This is Lilly," he said, nodding towards his fourteen year-old sister with the shoulder-length braided hair and thick-rimmed yet stylish glasses. "She'd shake your hand, but she's too much of a brat to actually pause a video game." She did pause it, most likely out of spite, and turned to shake Lexie's hand.

"Very funny," Lilly said. "He's just mad because I'm better at them than he is."

"That's because I don't waste as much time on them. I have a life."

"Oh yeah, playing nerd games on your iPad. What a life," she said, turning back to the screen and resuming her digital carnage.

"It's Words With Friends," he said to Lexie, holding up the pad. "She's mad because I beat everyone."

"Sounds fun," Lexie said, with a shrug of her shoulders. "I don't know that one."

"It's legally non-actionable Scrabble. Pretty much."

"Oh. Well, that could be fun. I'm mostly a crossword puzzle player, but I've played my share of that."

"Cool. You should get it and we can play."

"That could be fun. For you. Y'know, since you beat

everyone."

John chuckled. "Well, I can try to go easy on you. I guess."

The momentary silence was punctuated by more chainsaw sounds and zombie moans. Lexie realized her detour from awkwardness was just leading towards more of the same. "So you like basketball, huh?" she said, pointing at the wall.

"Yeah. Well, the Knicks. So I guess I'm more of a fan of heartbreak."

"Definitely," Lexie smiled. "I used to play in high school and sometimes I think I should head down there and teach them a thing or two.

John smiled back. "That'd be pretty cool. I'd love to see that."

"Oh my god," Lilly said, not turning around. "Are you flirting? Can I be embarrassed for you since you don't have the sense to do it yourself?"

"Oh fuck you!" John said, grabbing the pillow next to him and hurling it at the back of her head.

"Hey! Language!" Henry said, standing in the doorway.

"But Dad she--" John started, but Henry just put up a hand to quiet him.

"I heard. Lilly, that was rude. Stop that game and apologize."

With a drawn out groan, Lilly paused the game and turned around. "I'm sorry that my brother embarrassed himself."

"Lillian."

Another groan. "I'm sorry I was rude. To both of you. Can I play now please?"

"Only if you don't want cake," Henry said. "It's about to be cut."

The teenagers scrambled to their feet and squeezed past the two adults, John keeping his eyes averted from Lexie, who did her best to keep from smiling. Henry waited until they were down the hall before he shrugged and said, "Teenagers. What can you do?"

Lexie chuckled. "They're nice. I'm glad I finally got a chance to meet them."

Henry nodded. "Me too."

"Really?" she said, her voice taking on more of an edge than she intended.

Henry's brow furrowed. "Of course. What do you mean by that?"

"It's just--"

"Hey you two," Monica called, leaning into the hallway from the living room. "We can't cut the cake without the birthday boy."

"I've got him," Lexie said, heading down the hallway and giving Henry's arm a little pull. "C'mon, old man. I've got a powerful need for cake and alcohol."

As far as birthday parties went, Henry figured it was about as painless as it could get. He'd been worried that Lexie would find herself bored to tears among lawyers and their spouses, but despite the initial hiccups, it seemed she and Don were getting along rather well. Lilly quickly retreated back to her room, but John stayed and hovered around the outskirts of the conversations, including Lexie and Don's.

There was a buzz from the doorman, and Henry walked over to answer it.

"There's another guest on his way up, Mr. Churchill," the doorman said.

"Thanks, Manny," Henry said, looking over at Monica. She shrugged her shoulders, not knowing who it would be either. In the couple of minutes between the buzzer and the knock on the door, Henry managed to worry that one or more of the nearly dozen people he knew that he wouldn't want at his birthday party, let alone anywhere remotely near his family, had heard about it and decided to pay him a visit. While Monica was fully aware of the supernatural aspects of his business, he'd promised her that it would never find its way to their front door or threaten their family.

Every single unexpected buzz of the door, wrong number, or staring face in the crowd made him worry he was going to break that promise.

He hesitated for a moment before checking the peephole and then let out the breath he was holding.

"Richard, come in," Henry said, opening the door. "I thought Monica said you weren't going to be able to make it."

Richard Nichols nodded, stepping into the apartment. "Yeah, I've been a little under the weather, but I thought I'd at least stop in to say hello and pass on some birthday wishes." Richard was a junior associate at Monica's firm and was apparently on the fast track to be a junior partner. In his mid-thirties and usually the picture of health, Richard definitely looked ill. His skin was pale and he even seemed a bit smaller than normal, hunched over as if the act of standing was almost too much to bear.

"That's very nice of you," Henry said, gingerly taking the man's outstretched hand. At the touch Richard turned and coughed, covering his mouth with his other hand.

"Sorry," Rich said. "I guess I'm not as over this as I thought."

"Don't worry about it," Henry said, keeping a hold of the man's hand for another second before letting him go. "We've still got some cake left and Jane and Marcus haven't completely emptied the bar yet."

"Thanks," Rich said with his best attempt at a charming smile. He headed towards the other lawyers from the firm, meeting Monica on his way across the room. Henry watched, opening and closing the hand he'd shaken Rich's with while running the other over the close-cropped hair on his head.

"Everything okay?" Lexie said, walking up to him.

"Yeah. Just thinking."

"That's not a thinking look. That's a worried look."

Henry raised an eyebrow. "Oh really? You can tell the difference?"

Lexie smiled at him. "Let's just say you shouldn't take

up poker any time soon."

"So wait, where are we going?" Lexie said.

It'd been nearly two weeks since Henry's birthday party, and the two were in the company car heading back uptown near Greenwich Village after a meeting with one of their mundane clients, a mid-level banking firm they did regular background checks for.

"I just want to make a stop before we head back to the office," Henry said.

"Obviously, but a stop where? And even better, why?"

Henry sighed. "I wanted to check in on one of the lawyers at Monica's firm. He's called in sick the past couple of days and I wanted to see if he's okay."

"Huh. That's sweet. I guess. Can't you just give him a call?"

"It's complicated."

Lexie crossed her arms and studied him. "Who is it? The smarmy little preppy one that looked like death warmed over at your party?"

Henry smiled. "Yes. Him. He worked at the firm for almost five years and he's never taken a sick day in his life. Now

Monica says it's gotten worse. His work has been suffering and he's even missed a couple of court dates."

"People get sick, Henry. It happens."

"True, but usually young hotshots like this fight their way through it unless they're physically incapable of moving. If they can't, then they go to the hospital. When Monica spoke to him today she told him to go see a doctor, but he refused. Said he was being taken care of."

"This all sounds completely reasonable. Unless . . . you had that look on your face when he came to the party. That 'there's something afoot' face."

"What?"

"In all the time we've worked together, we've never ended up on a case that we thought would be all extraordinary and spooky but turned out to be a hoax or a joke or a waste of time. You've turned away people that have seemed totally legit, but helped others that have seemed like total loons. Right before we take the one of those spook cases you get that look on your face."

"Spook cases?" he said.

"We don't exactly have a technical term, and stop dodging the question. You can tell somehow, can't you? If someone's been . . . well, spooked."

He grinned a little as they pulled into a parking spot. "The supernatural tends to leave a mark, like an aftertaste, on the world. When you've been doing this awhile you can almost begin to sense it. If you've used enough magic, you can sometimes even tell just by touching someone."

"That's cheating," she said, getting out of the car.

"Would you rather we had to follow up with every unstable person that walks through the door?" he said, taking a plastic grocery bag out from the backseat of the car and following suit.

"Only if their checks clear. And don't think I haven't noticed that some of the cases we do end up taking don't pay as well as the non-spooky ones."

They walked up the steps to Rich's building, a fancy, two-story brownstone on a quiet side street, and Henry rang the bell. "Now that would be cheating," he said.

"Whatever. I just don't want you to tell me one day that we're out of money. Some of us don't have a pretty lawyer wife to be the breadwinner in case of emergencies."

Henry turned and looked at her, and Lexie regretted the edge her voice had taken. "I also have two children, one about to go to college and the other right on his heels. I can assure you I'm just as worried about money as you are."

Before Lexie could respond, the intercom crackled with Rich's voice. "Hello?"

"Richard, it's Henry Churchill. Monica said you haven't been feeling well so I figured I'd bring you some stuff to maybe help you out."

There was a long pause before Richard responded. "Okay. That's . . . that's very nice of you." It could have been just the intercom, but Rich's voice sounded thin and weak. He buzzed them up and they walked in, heading up the stairs to the second floor. At the top the door was cracked, and she could see Richard staring at them through it, the chain on the door still on and a blanket wrapped around his shoulders.

"How are you feeling?" Henry asked as they reached the door.

"Been better," he said, turning and coughing. Even through the gap in the door, Lexie could see that he looked far worse than he did at the party. His skin was paler, nearly gray, and hung off of him as if he'd lost weight suddenly. "Thanks for checking in, but it really isn't necessary."

"My pleasure. You know how everyone at the firm is,

one big happy family."

Richard nodded, and after a moment Henry held up the plastic bag he'd been carrying. "Can we come in? I don't think this will fit through the crack there."

"Oh. Right. Sure. Hold on." Rich closed the door, and after a few moments they could hear him fumbling with the chain. For a second, Lexie thought it sounded like he was saying something, but the door opened before she could ask if Henry heard it too.

Richard's apartment was large and modern. Big open spaces where a living room in the front flowed into a dining area, and then the kitchen was divided from the rest of the apartment by only a long, waist-high counter. Past the kitchen was a short hallway leading to the back of the apartment. She could tell from Henry's face that he'd also heard the soft footfalls disappearing into the back.

"Is there someone here?" he asked, walking the bag over to the kitchen counter.

She could tell from the almost panicked look on Richard's face that there was, but he just shook his head as he forced out another cough to hide it. "No," he said weakly. "Probably just my cat."

"No kidding," Lexie said, walking towards the living room. "I'm deathly allergic. Flare right up, sneezing and coughing if there's one anywhere around me." She took a deep breath and smiled at him. "But here I am, right as rain. How about that?"

Richard winced and then coughed for real this time. "She's a short hair. Hypoallergenic."

"No shit," Lexie said, looking into the living room. "I didn't think that was a real thing." The living room looked as if it were normally sleek and pristine, with black and chrome electronics and tidy bookshelves, but it appeared to be in complete disarray. Most notably, the couch had dirty sheets on it and the chair and floor next to it had piles of clothes, far more than just a couple of sick day's worth.

"Yeah, it is." he said, trying to move between her and the rest of the apartment, but shuffling slowly as if lifting his legs were too much of an effort.

"What's her name?"

"Who?" he said.

"The cat," Lexie said, stepping towards him. On a day where Richard was well, he would've been eye to eye with Lexie's nearly six feet but today, slumped from sickness, she practically towered over him. "What's the cat's name?"

"Oh. Right." Fake cough again. "Um. May. Her name's May."

"Weird name for a cat," she said, stepping forward again. Richard stepped back this time.

"Okay," Henry called from the kitchen. "I've got you all set up here. Some chicken soup, some orange juice, and even a little tea. I've found it can work wonders." Richard turned and shuffled back towards him as Henry opened the refrigerator to put in the groceries he'd bought. "Huh," Henry said, looking at the nearly empty shelves. "Maybe I should go get you some more stuff."

"I'm fine," Richard said, his voice taking on an edge of panic. "I can get stuff later, I just . . . I think I'm very contagious. I don't want you to get sick."

"Yeah," Lexie said, circling around him. "Summer colds are the worst."

Richard nodded, heading towards the front door. "Yeah. It's terrible, so you should just . . . go, okay? Please?"

Henry walked over to Richard and stared at him, finally putting a hand on his shoulder. The younger man flinched but didn't move. "Are you okay, Richard? Are you sure you don't need anything?"

Richard nodded. "Yeah. I'm sure I'll be fine."

She could see Henry concentrating as he stared at Richard, finally saying, "If you're in trouble I can help you. No matter what it is, no matter how strange it may be, we can help you."

After a confused look, Richard shook his head vigorously, so much so that he would've fallen over if Henry hadn't been holding him. "I'm fine. I'm just sick, that's all." Henry stared a bit longer and then let go.

"Okay. Well, maybe we'll be back to check up on you later."

"It's really not necessary," he said, opening the door for them.

"It's really no bother," Henry said, stepping out into the hallway and waving for Lexie to follow.

"Really?" she said. "That's it?"

"Yeah. C'mon, Richard needs his rest."

She shrugged her shoulders and followed after him, Richard practically closed the door on her as she left. Halfway down the stairs she said, "Are you serious? That guy is lying through his teeth."

Henry nodded. "About everything but being sick. There's definitely something wrong with him, but it sure as hell isn't the flu."

"Something spooky?" she said with a smile.

"Yeah," he said, heading out onto the street. "You could say that. He's hiding something, but he doesn't really think he's in any danger. Which means he's probably in more danger than I thought."

"You could say that," a female voice came from behind them as they reached the car. Lexie turned to see a woman in her late twenties, possibly early thirties, with shoulder-length red hair and in a t-shirt, jeans, and light jacket, staring at them through aviator sunglasses. It was too warm out for the jacket, but Lexie realized that the woman was likely wearing it for the same reason that she was wearing hers: she was armed.

Lexie's hand drifted back towards the holstered Walther clipped to the small of her back, but the woman shook her head and pulled her jacket to the side to reveal her own pistol. "I wouldn't, Miss. Susan York, Immigration and Customs Enforcement. You need to tell me what you know about Richard Nichols and what you think he's hiding up there."

"Or what?" Henry said, coming back around from the driver's side with his hands relaxed but opened at his sides. "What is it that you think he's hiding up there?"

"An illegal," she said. "And a murderer. Which makes you both accessories if you don't tell me what you know right now."

It took some doing, but Henry convinced Susan that they could all sit down at the restaurant at the corner and share what they both knew without any more threats or weapons being drawn.

"So you're P.I.s?" Susan said, eyeing them both. "You look like the goddamn odd couple."

"We get that a lot," Lexie said.

"Richard works with my wife at Kendall, Brown, and Churchill," Henry said. "He's been sick, but I think it's more than that."

"More than sick? Yeah, you could say that. Near as I can tell, your pal up there is harboring an illegal that got away from me on a raid and may have been involved in a murder. I've been watching his place for weeks, but I think he's on to me. He hasn't left the house in nearly a week."

"What makes you think that?" Lexie said. Susan narrowed her eyes at Lexie and then looked away.

"About four months ago my partner and I raided a building in Chinatown that was harboring illegals. Everything went fine until we found a group of girls hiding out in the basement. We thought we'd gotten them all out, but my partner Bonnie found something and . . ." she trailed off, drumming her fingers on the table and staring down into her coffee.

"She died," she finally said. "There was a room, a sealed up room that, like an idiot, she opened on her own rather than waiting for me, and someone in there killed her. Slashed her across the throat and ran."

"Did you see what it was?" Henry asked.

"What do you mean what? It was someone locked in that room, and when she let them out they killed her. It was dark. They took out the lights, and in the chaos that happened some of the girls that were kept in that cellar got away through the access to the street. It was a complete and total clusterfuck, and we don't have anything to show for it except for a handful of illegals and some gambling charges."

"So how does Richard fit into this?" Lexie asked.

"He's their lawyer, isn't he?" Henry answered.

"Bingo," Susan said with a snarl. "The scumbags that own that building hired your wife's firm to defend them, and damn if they weren't doing a fine job of it until about a month ago. That's when Richard started getting all squirrelly and holding up in his apartment claiming to be sick."

"He's sick all right," Henry said. "And you can't really blame him for doing his job."

"I can't? He's defending a couple of scumbags who were in human trafficking and keeping someone locked up in a sealed room. This is pretty cut and dried, but he's been working wonders for them."

Henry nodded. "Richard has worked a lot on immigration cases, especially when it comes to China."

"Oh you don't have to tell me," Susan said. "Richie was in the top five percent of his class at Rutgers, graduating from law school in 2004 and is nearly fluent in Chinese. Family that's practically one percenters. He's been squeaky clean until now."

"If you're so sure that he's got someone up there with him," Lexie said, "then why don't you just get a warrant and search the place?"

Susan grimaced and took a drink of her coffee.

"You can't, can you?" Henry said. "You never did show us your credentials, agent. Or is it former agent?"

"I'm on administrative leave. They're concerned that I'm not thinking clearly with regards to the death of my partner. Among other things."

"Fantastic," Lexie said. "So what, you've been stalking this guy on your off time?"

"Yeah, I have," she snapped. "Because everyone else is doing fuck-all about Bonnie's death. At least two of the girls that were down in that cellar got away in all the confusion, not to mention whoever was in that room. If Richie is harboring one of them, which you two seem to be confirming, then I'm going to go up there and find out what they know. One way or another."

Her outburst drew some looks from the rest of the lunch crowd, and Henry held up a hand to try to calm her down. "Okay, I get that. I do, but I think there's more going on here than you realize. We can help you and Richard and find out who killed your partner without resorting to extreme--"

"--and illegal," Lexie interrupted.

"Yes, illegal methods," he finished. "We may even be able to do it in a way that saves you from any further trouble.

Will you let us?"

Susan looked from one to the other and then nodded. "Okay. One chance."

"Good," Henry said. "Before we go back up there, take me to the building where all this happened."

It took some doing, but Henry convinced the building's manager, a tiny, perpetually nervous man named Eric Chen, to let them see the cellar where Bonnie Walters had died.

"We didn't do anything wrong," he said to them as they walked down the steps. "There wasn't anyone down there."

Lexie pulled Susan along before she could turn and yell back. "That piece of shit," Susan grumbled.

"Did the girls that didn't get away say they were mistreated?" Lexie asked.

"No, but what they did say didn't make any sense either."

Henry stopped at the foot of the stairs. "What did they say?"

"They said that they were afraid of one of the other girls that came with them. Even after she died."

"That's not good, is it?" Lexie asked him.

"Probably not," Henry said, opening the door. Whatever had been broken four months ago was now repaired, as the cellar was well-lit and practically empty aside from a few boxes. Susan stopped in the doorway, taking it all in.

"Down there," she said, pointing towards the far corner of the room. Henry nodded and headed towards it, but Lexie stayed behind with Susan.

"I'm sorry about your partner," she said.

"You and me both," Susan said, not looking at Lexie but staring into the room, probably at the spot where she watched her partner die. After a couple of moments, Susan reached up and wiped a tear from her eye.

"How long did you work together?"

"We were in the same office for about three years, but we were together for almost two."

"Ah," Lexie said. "When you said partner, I didn't think you meant like that. That makes it even worse."

"You're telling me. We tried to keep it under wraps, but after this it was hard. It's part of the reason they put me on leave."

"That sucks," Lexie said. "They didn't repeal DADT

until I was out of the service. Not that I had many opportunities, but it would've been nice to have the option."

Susan looked over at her, but before she could say anything Henry called them over. "Do you want to stay here?" Lexie asked, but Susan just shook her head. In the back corner of the room was a door standing open, and just inside Henry walked in a slow circle. The room was small, only about twenty feet square, and was lit only by the lights from the adjoining room. As near as Lexie could tell, the door was made of some sort of metal and on the inside there were several deep scratches in groups of four.

"Fuck's sake," Susan said, kneeling down to get a closer look at them. "This is metal. What the hell could they have used to leave scratches like these?"

"Not what," Henry said. "Who. Whoever they had locked up in here."

"That's nuts," Susan said, standing up and looking around.

"Tell me those don't look like claw marks to you," Lexie said, pointing at the door. "What was it?" she asked Henry. "Some kind of werewolf?"

"Oh give me a break!" Susan said. "Those may look like

fingers or claws or whatever, but it wasn't some damn werewolf! It was the middle of the afternoon when we got here!"

"So what was it?" Henry asked her. "Something was in this room, something unnatural, and they knew it. The only way they knew how to deal with it was to lock it up." Henry stepped out of the room and shined his light on the outside of the door. "These markings, what do they say?" he asked Susan.

"Nothing," she said, coming around to look. "I studied them after, but they're just gibberish."

"I think it's some kind of spell. Something they put in place to keep whatever they had in there from being able to break out." Henry reached out and peeled away one of the pieces of paper and tucked it into his pocket.

"Look, I gave you two the benefit of the doubt, but now you're just pissing me off. What is this, some kind of diversion while Nichols makes his escape?" Susan said, heading for the stairs.

Henry and Lexie followed her. "No, it's not that," he called after her. "I think whatever was in that room killed your partner and is still on the loose. It might even be what's making Richard sick." They didn't catch Susan until she reached the top of the stairs, the building manager still waiting with a nervous and pained expression on his face.

"Wait," Lexie said, grabbing Susan's arm before she pushed past him. "Just hear us out, okay? I know this stuff seems nuts, but something you can't explain happened down there, right? Something killed Bonnie and made its way past everyone, and you didn't even see what it was. Does that make any sense to you?"

Susan stopped, pulling herself free of Lexie's grip but not making any further moves to leave. After a couple of seconds she turned around to face her. "No, it doesn't. I've thought about that day nearly every waking hour for the past four months, and nothing about it makes sense. But you can't seriously believe that some monster was down there, can you?"

"I do. It's a crazy world out there," Lexie said. "Monsters, ghosts. You'd be surprised at what's real."

"This is too much," Mr. Chen said, putting his hands up in the air. "You've seen enough so just please go, okay?"

"Wait, please," Henry said, putting his hand on the man's shoulder. "Mr. Chen, wasn't it? I just want to know what was in the room. You're not in trouble."

"Not yet," Susan said, narrowing her eyes at him when he turned to look at her.

Henry reached into the pocket of his jacket, and when Mr. Chen turned back Henry had a half-dollar sized coin held up in front of his face. "What is . . . " Mr. Chen started, but trailed off as Henry began to flip the coin between his fingers. The light reflected off it as it moved and flickered across Mr. Chen's face.

"What is he doing?" Susan asked Lexie, who moved to block what was happening in the hallway from anyone looking in from the restaurant's kitchen.

"Don't worry," Lexie said softly. "It's just some light hypnosis."

"I don't think hypnosis works that way."

"True, but whatever it is, it gets the job done," Lexie said, nodding at Mr. Chen. The man's face had gone slack, and it seemed like the man might have fallen over half-asleep if Henry didn't have a hand on his shoulder still.

"Mr. Chen," Henry said in a soothing voice that even made Lexie feel a little drowsy. "What was down there in that room?"

"I don't know," he said in an equally calm voice. "It's just for storage, but they said they had something they needed to keep down there, no questions asked."

"Who's they?" Henry asked.

"The ones who bring people to this country. We don't hurt them, just give them jobs and a place to stay. This time was different, though."

"Why was it different?"

"They said something happened on the way here from China. They didn't know what to do, but someone came and told them to lock it away in the room. So they did, even though they were scared."

"Who told them?"

Mr. Chen's brow crinkled in confusion. "I don't remember."

"It's okay, don't worry about it," Henry said, and Mr. Chen's face relaxed again. "Why were they scared?"

"They said one of the girls died just before she got here. That she was sick, but they were afraid still."

"Did they think they were going to get sick?" Henry asked.

"No, they were afraid of her. They said she was cursed."

"What did they put down there?"

His face tensed again but then relaxed. "I don't know,

but one of the busboys saw them put it down there and that it looked like . . . like a body."

"There's no way," Susan said. "They told me they went over every inch of that room, and nothing was in there, especially not a dead body. There would've been DNA everywhere, not to mention the smell."

"It may have been a body, but it may not have been dead," Henry said, not looking at her but keeping his focus on Mr. Chen. "What did they call it?" he asked Chen. "They had a name for it, didn't they?"

"I'm not sure."

"Did they say anything strange? Anything out of the ordinary?"

"Someone said *huli jing*. I don't know what that is."

It was Henry's turn to contort his face with worry. "Okay, good. What about the lawyer? What happened when he came here?"

"When he showed up, we told him that one of the girls had gotten away from immigration and she was staying with another family. He said he could help her, but that it wasn't safe with them so he would take care of her." Mr. Chen grimaced. "I didn't like the way he looked at her. The family didn't want the girl to stay with them anymore. They had heard what had happened, and they were scared too. So she went with him."

"Okay. Thank you, Mr. Chen." Henry pocketed the coin and took his hand off of the man's shoulder. Mr. Chen straightened up and then yawned, blinking a little as he looked around the room.

"What?" he said, unsure what to make of Susan's staring at him.

"Nothing," Henry said. "I think we're all set here, Mr. Chen. Thanks again." He nodded at Lexie and the two headed for the exit.

"That's it?" Susan said, calling after them as she followed.

"We know what we're dealing with now," Henry said over his shoulder. "Now we just have to figure out how to stop it."

"A fox spirit?" Susan said from the back seat, leaning up against the back of Lexie's chair. "Like, a ghost?"

"Basically," Henry said, pulling into a parking spot down the block from Richard's apartment. "Some legends say it's a fox that's turned into a human. Others that it's a spirit looking for revenge. There are similar fox stories in Korea and Japan, but in almost all cases the spirit can make itself appear in human or fox form, and it drains the life force from a victim."

"Like a vampire?" Lexie asked.

"More like a succubus," Henry said.

Susan put her fist on her forehead and closed her eyes. "This is so stupid."

Lexie turned around. "You said yourself that you couldn't think of any other explanation as to what had happened down there. I know it seems crazy, but just trust us, okay? I promise you that we will take care of the thing that killed Bonnie."

Susan opened her eyes and gave Lexie a weak smile. "It's not like I have any other choice. So a succubus, right? That's some kind of sex demon or something, isn't it?"

Henry nodded. "Basically."

"Ew," Lexie said. "So he offered to hide this girl just so he could nail her? Gross."

"We don't know that for sure," Henry said. "The spirit may have charmed him, seeing him as a way to escape. It's probably still weak from being imprisoned."

"I don't know," Lexie said. "Did you see how Richie looked like he was ready to fall right over? If it's been feeding off of him it must be good and ripe by now."

"Either way we can't wait much longer," Henry said, getting out of the car. Lexie and Susan followed him down the block. "Remember," Henry said, looking back at Susan, "this thing is a shapeshifter. And dangerous. Just follow our lead."

"Yeah, whatever," Susan said. Henry buzzed up and they waited until Richard called down.

"It's Henry Churchill again, Richard. I've got some more stuff for you."

Even through the intercom they could hear Richard's exhausted sigh. "That's really okay, Henry. I should be fine for now."

"I'm sure you are," Henry said, "but I also have something I need to talk you about."

"Can't it wait? I'm really tired right now."

"I don't think it can," Henry said. "I need your help with something."

There was a long pause and then the door buzzed open. The three walked up the steps, and Richard was waiting for them in his doorway. "Who's that?" he said, motioning to

Susan.

"A friend of ours," Henry said. "She needed our help with something. Can we come in?"

Richard looked back into his apartment and then nodded, holding the door open for them.

"I thought you said you had something for me," Richard said, closing the door behind them.

"I do," Henry said, reaching into his jacket pocket and taking out one of the slips of paper that had been pasted to the basement cell door and holding it out for Richard to see. "Ring any bells?"

Lexie didn't think it was possible for Richard to get any paler but he did. "Look, I don't know what you think--"

"We know all about your house guest, asshole," Susan interrupted. "So why don't you come on out!" She yelled the last bit and Lexie threw her hands up in frustration.

"Does, 'follow our lead,' mean anything to you?" she said, walking quickly towards the hallway in the back of the apartment, hand reaching back for her gun. She only made it a couple of steps before a young Chinese woman, probably just eighteen or nineteen, cautiously stepped out from the hallway.

"Richard, is everything okay?" she said in slow and

accented English.

"I take it this is your cat, May, huh?" Lexie said, stopping but keeping her hand behind her back and near her gun.

"Yes, but it's not what you think," Richard said, taking a couple of steps towards her but stopping to cough so violently he almost fell to the ground.

"Actually," Henry said, stepping forward to help him, "it's not what you think. May, can you come in here please?"

Before she could take a step, Susan drew her gun and pointed it at the young woman. "Actually, May, don't move."

"Susan, come on!" Lexie said, stepping between the two. "Just relax."

"Screw that," Susan said. "That girl is either an illegal being harbored by that scumbag or she's not even a girl at all. She's either coming with me and getting deported or I'm putting this fox girl down for good."

"Fox girl?" Richard said. "What the hell are you talking about?"

"It's complicated," Henry said, leading Richard to a chair in the living room. "But I need you to stay here and for everyone else to calm down."

"I assure you I am very calm," Susan said, stepping to the side to try to get a clean line of fire on May.

"I know you are," Lexie said, turning and keeping her body in the line of fire as she looked back and forth from May to Susan. "But this could just be an innocent kid. You need to let us figure this out. Henry, anytime you want to help with that figuring it out thing, just jump right in here."

Henry stepped forward and put a hand out towards May, closing his eyes. "Working on it," he said, frowning in concentration. Susan continued to circle around, aiming at the trembling young woman. Susan was now standing in the kitchen area and May had shifted nearer to the front door of the apartment, looking in terror at the gun pointed at her. When she realized where she was she began to shuffle towards the door.

"Don't you dare," Susan said, stepping to the side again with her back to the hallway and the rest of the apartment.

"It's not her," Henry said, opening his eyes. "There's something, but it's not her." May turned to look at Henry who came towards her, hands up but still holding the scrap of paper with the spell-script on it. "It's okay," he said, reaching out to her with it in his hand. "See?" He placed the paper on her shoulder, and even though she leaned away from him in confusion, it had no other effect. "If she was the *huli jing* it'd harm her."

At the mention of the spirit, May's eyes opened wide. "No! I am not! She is evil!"

"Thanks, kid," Lexie said. "We figured that part out." She turned to Susan. "See? She's just a scared kid. Now put that down and we can get to the bottom of this."

"No way," Susan snarled. "You two were just full of shit with all your ridiculous talk of fox ghosts and all that other nonsense. I am bringing that girl in and she's going to tell me who killed Bonnie. Now get out of the way."

Lexie took a step towards Susan, taking her hand off her gun and holding it up with the other one. "I just want you to calm down, okay? I know it hurts to lose someone, but we can help. Just take a breath, put the gun down, and we can talk."

"There isn't anything to talk about. Bonnie's dead and she's never coming back, but I can at least bring one of the people responsible to justice. None of your ghost stories can fix that."

"You'd be surprised," Lexie said. "I know what it's like

to miss something. I miss my old life every day. I live in a big city without any friends and a job that's so weird I don't know how I'll ever make any, let alone find what you and Bonnie had. I know that's not the same as losing someone you love, but I get it, I really do. But I also know that you can't fix it this way. Just put the gun down before you do something . . . " Lexie trailed off, looking over Susan's shoulder. "Holy crap, Susan look out."

Susan rolled her eyes. "What are you, eleven? That's not going to work." Right as she said that Lexie could tell that Susan heard the scuff of the footsteps behind her from the other girl coming towards them from the hallway. Susan turned around just in time to see the second girl emerge into the light and realize that she didn't just look like May, but was identical to her. Same pretty face, same long hair, and same simple, floral dress.

But this May was growling, her face contorted in a snarl.

The real May gasped, backing up into Henry who moved the young girl behind him. Susan took several steps back, swinging her gun around at the new arrival. "Wait, who's that?" Richard called weakly from the living room.

"The problem," Lexie said, stepping back as well and

drawing her Walther. "Eaaaaaaaasy there, girl. Bad dog."

The growling May looked around the room, her gaze stopping on the two guns pointed at it. "Go away," it snarled.

"Oh good, it speaks English," Lexie said.

"We hear English," Henry said, stepping towards them.

"Leave her alone," the second May said. It had copied May's body perfectly, but the voice was deep and thick, the animalistic growl coming through.

"Leave who alone?" Henry asked, inching closer.

The spirit's eyes moved over to May, who was now sitting next to Richard. Both looked absolutely terrified. Henry glanced back at them. "Why? Who is she to you?"

The spirit snarled again. "She is my friend. I keep her safe."

Behind them May gasped and shook her head furiously. "No! No! You are bad! Demon! Monster!"

For a second the spirit stopped growling and its face softened. It stepped back and its form began to shimmer. May's features melted away, the spirit became shorter and heavier, its hair retracted up until it was shoulder-length, and left a completely different girl standing in front of them. "It's me," the spirit said in the same deep, growling voice. "I'm your friend. I said I'd look after you when we got to America and I meant it."

May shrieked and turned away, violently shaking her head. "No! Bao is dead! She is gone! You are a monster!"

"It's about to be a dead monster," Susan said, but before she could do anything the spirit turned to look at her. Bao's form melted away and it became taller, blonder, and white. Susan's gun trembled and lowered slightly. "Bonnie?" she said.

"Hey, beautiful," the thing said, the animalistic growl gone from its voice. "I'm so happy you found me. I was so scared."

"I thought . . . " Susan's gun lowered some more as she trailed off, taking a step towards her.

"Susan!" Lexie yelled. "That's not her! It's a trick!"

"It's done something to her," Henry said, standing at Lexie's side.

Susan's gun arm dropped and she reached out for her dead girlfriend. "I missed you," she whispered. "I missed you so much." The spirit reached out for her.

"Susan, wake up!" Lexie screamed, leaping towards

them. The spirit darted forward with a snarl, grabbed Susan's outstretched arm, and tossed her at Lexie. The two women collided and flew backwards into the kitchen counter, dropping their guns. The *huli jing* growled through suddenly sharp teeth like an angry animal, fingertips extending to claws and face narrowing into a snout with a hint of copper and white fur as it closed on the still stunned Lexie and Susan.

Henry raised the sheet with the spell script on it and spoke unrecognizable words. The script on the paper began to glow and the creature backed off from the light. Susan shook her head, and when she realized what she was seeing, she leapt for the gun laying between them.

With a rough bark the thing swiped at her hand with its claws, slashing the top of her hand and sending blood spraying across the floor. Susan recoiled with a yell and the creature, now looking like a humanoid fox complete with ears and fur, squatted down to pounce on them. Lexie dove forward before it could, tackling the creature and pushing it backwards and off balance, but it stayed on its feet, the claws on its toes digging into the tile of the kitchen floor.

With a roar it grabbed Lexie's back, dug its claws into her, and lifted her off the ground. Lexie clenched her jaw, thankful her jacket and shirt were taking most of the edge off the claws. She tried to get a grip on the thing's fur, but it stood up straight, turned, and then slammed her into the ground.

Lexie was stunned from the impact, but managed to get her forearm up just as the thing's jaws came down towards her face. The teeth sank into her forearm, and this time her jacket didn't provide much help. Blood flowed down her forearm as the thing shook its head with her arm still in its mouth. Lexie gritted her own teeth, refusing to cry out as she batted away the paw that wasn't holding her down.

Blood was dripping onto her chest, and the spirit began to pull upwards while still pinning her to the ground with its paws, digging its teeth in deeper. Before she could give in and scream, Henry was there behind it, still chanting and placing the glowing piece of paper on the thing's back. It let go of her arm to howl in pain and reared up, pushing Henry off of it.

"Oh, no you don't," Lexie said, reaching up and grabbing the thing by one of its ears. She pulled its head to the side and pushed up, rolling the spirit onto its back and holding it down. Henry reached past her and placed the paper on the thing's chest and began to chant louder. The paper glowed and the spirit howled in pain as it thrashed on the kitchen floor. Susan grabbed it from the other side and pinned its other arm down as Henry continued the spell. The struggle grew weaker and weaker, and its animal features began to fade, looking like Bao once more.

This time, however, she looked sick and weak. Probably like she did right before she died. "I wanted to protect her," the thing said, its voice weak. "We were going to take care of each other in America."

Henry's voice got softer and then the sick girl beneath them vanished in a cloud of smoke. Lexie dropped to the floor, holding her injured arm against her chest as she rolled onto her back. "I hate to reinforce stereotypes," she said through gritted teeth, "but this is why I'm a cat person."

"I don't understand," Richard said, shaking his head. It had only been about fifteen minutes, but he already looked better. Henry figured it'd only be a matter of hours before he was back to his old self.

"The *huli jing* was trying to protect May," Henry said. "The two girls met on the voyage over before Bao got sick. She must have cared so much that she wanted to protect her even after she died. Some families have ties to the supernatural, and if one of them dies unexpectedly or there's some kind of lingering connection, it can cause a transformation like this."

"Protect her from what?" Richard said. "I wasn't trying to hurt anyone. I just wanted to help her stay in this country."

"Really?" Lexie said, wincing as Susan tied the bandage around her arm. The bites had been deep but thankfully didn't hit any arteries. Lexie was more relieved that she wasn't going to turn into a fox herself and become a, 'living Jimi Hendrix song,' as she put it.

"Yeah," Susan said. "That thing didn't drain your life force just by shaking hands."

Henry raised an eyebrow at him and Richard blushed, looking down into his coffee. "I just . . . she was so pretty and I wanted to help her. I didn't think . . . " he looked over at May, who sat quietly on the far end of the couch, not looking at him.

"I let her stay in my room, and I slept on the couch. I thought she was just being shy. She said that she liked me," Richard said, his voice taking on a pleading tone as he stared at May. She shook her head.

"Not like that," she said. "You were nice to me and not scared like everyone else. You helped me learn more English, and you said you were going to help me stay in this country, and I was happy. But I did not want that."

"I thought it was her," Richard said, looking away. "She would come in the middle of the night and she . . . I just thought that was the only way she was comfortable with me, and that she just needed some time to get used to me and then we could be together, for real. I didn't do anything wrong."

"Just harbor an illegal alien," Susan said, getting to her feet.

"And be kind of gross," Lexie said, flexing her wounded arm with a wince.

"I was lonely," he said. "I thought I'd found someone that needed me and could fix that." He looked up at Lexie. "You said yourself that you knew what it was like."

"I do, but that doesn't mean I'm going to do something stupid and illegal to fix it. Did I mention gross? Because your little damsel in distress fantasy was kind of gross."

Richard looked down again and Susan gave a sigh. "Look," she said. "I don't have to say you were involved, but I do have to take May in."

"Are you sure?" Henry said. "I may know some folks that can help her."

"Yeah, I'm sure. It may make me look more like a crazy person to my boss, and I have no idea how I'm going to explain it, but yeah. That's non-negotiable."

Lexie knocked on Susan's window before she drove away. Susan rolled it down and Lexie leaned in. "Are you sure I can't change your mind?"

"Yeah. I appreciate your helping me and opening up, but this is still my job."

"Fair enough," Lexie said, wincing as she reached into her pocket for a business card. "If you need anything, feel free to give me a call."

Susan took it with her bandaged hand and a slight hint of a smile. "I may do that at some point. Not right away, you know. But someday."

"I completely understand," Lexie said. "Even if it's just to talk."

Susan rolled up the window and drove away. Henry walked up to Lexie as they watched the car drive away. "Did you just give your number to someone that's basically a widow?"

"Shut up," she said, walking towards their car without looking at him. "It was just business. And stuff. Plus shut up."

She got behind the wheel, and when he got in the little smirk on his face was gone.

"I'm sorry. I didn't realize that you felt so . . . isolated."

"Ugh, you did hear all that, didn't you? I opened up and it was gross and let's not talk about it again, okay?"

"Okay," he said. "But let me just say that you're not entirely alone. I know it's a big city and it can be intimidating, but I consider you a friend. I hope you feel the same."

"Fine, let's just keep talking about it anyway," she said, taking the key out of the ignition. "I'm your friend, huh? Is that why you never say anything about your family? That I met your wife twice and your kids once in nine months? I didn't even know if they knew what we really do most of the time until that party! You're like a sphinx, always keeping secrets!"

"I don't think that's what sphinxes--"

"No!" She said, jabbing a finger at him. "Don't change the subject! You wanted to talk about my little emotional hiccup, so let's talk about it. Secrets! You! Constantly!"

Henry sighed. "Okay. You're right, I don't talk about my kids or my wife because I've seen what's happened to people who have been in this world and tried to have both. It's dangerous and scary and usually something has to give. Monica knows about this world and this life, but I've been trying to make sure my kids never know. I just want them to go to college, grow up, and have normal lives. I worry about something from this life coming after them every second of every day. That's why I don't have any pictures of them or even talk about them in the office. Sometimes you never know who's listening."

Lexie nodded. "Okay, fine. That . . . well, that makes a lot of sense and I guess I feel a little silly now."

Henry shook his head. "No, it's my fault. I should've told you about this. Trusted you more."

"You don't trust me?" she said.

"No, I do. It just took a little bit of time, and then I just didn't want to bring it up. That's my fault and I'm sorry."

Lexie nodded and put the key in the ignition. "Okay. Fair enough. Now can we never talk about this emotional grossness again?"

Henry smiled. "Deal."

She drove them back to the office in silence. She parked the car in the garage, and the two of them began to walk towards their respective homes after saying quiet goodbyes.

"Hey," Henry called after her. Lexie stopped and

waited for him to catch up. "Do you want to come over for dinner? Monica is making meatloaf, which is actually really good. Plus I'm sure the kids would want to see you again."

Lexie smiled. "Sounds good. But can you tell John I like girls before I have to have another conversation with a boy about inappropriate affection?"

"Fair enough," he said with a smile, taking out his phone. He looked down and frowned at it.

"What is it?" Lexie asked.

"Just a missed call," he said, putting it to his ear and listening to the message. She watched him frown and then begin dialing home.

"Who was it?" she asked.

"Nothing to worry about," he said.

"Really? After what we just talked about?"

"Trust me," he said. "This is nothing you want to deal with."

"It seems like the more I do this job, the longer that list gets."

Henry gave a grim little smile. "Eventually that's all it becomes."

A couple of days later, Henry walked into a bar near the office after he and Lexie had finished for the day. He stopped in the doorway, looked for the person he was meeting, and saw him sitting in the back at a table by himself. He walked over and sat. As he did, the young man looked up from the cell phone that had been monopolizing his attention.

"Mr. Green, nice to see you again," Henry said.

"Yeah, it's nice to see you too. I guess," Martin Green mumbled. Almost two months ago, Martin found himself tricked by a demon he'd summoned into transforming himself into a monstrous, ape-like creature bent on killing an ex-girlfriend. The experience had left the young man rattled, and Henry could understand that he wasn't too thrilled to be reminded of it, especially given the voice mail he'd left for Henry. Henry had tried in the weeks after Martin's encounter to get in touch with him, but the young man hadn't returned any of his calls until the other day.

"I'm sorry if this is difficult for you," Henry said.

"Yeah, I know," Martin sat up, running a hand through his slightly curly, black hair. He looked a little better than the first and only time Henry had seen him, but given he'd just returned to his human form at the time, that wasn't exactly a high benchmark to meet. Still, he looked harried and exhausted, several days unshaven and with bags under his eyes. "Then again," Martin continued, "the whole fucking thing is my fault anyway so I guess I should man up and accept it, huh?"

Henry nodded. "To a certain extent, yes. I can assure you though that people make mistakes all the time, especially when it comes to things like this. The supernatural world is . . . seductive. A lot of times people think it comes with easy answers and quick fixes, but it never does. There's always a price."

Martin chuckled without much amusement. "You're telling me. I lost my job after being gone for days and not being able to explain it, I can't afford my apartment any more and now I don't even want to go back there because I'm so freaked out. Do you know how hard it is to scrub a summoning circle painted in blood off your floor?"

"Actually, yes."

Martin smiled with sincerity this time. "Yeah, I bet you do. It wasn't just the fact that I had a demon in my house or what I did to get it there that got me spooked. After I got that message I didn't even want to go back there again. I've been crashing with my parents in Jersey which, I can assure you, is almost as bad."

"Can I see it?" Henry asked.

Martin nodded, turning on the screen and sliding his phone across the table. "I haven't been able to stop looking at it since I got it."

Henry picked it up and looked at the text message that was listed as being from, "A Friend." It read:

Sorry that things didn't work out for you. I hope that you aren't too disappointed or angry but it seemed like it was something you really wanted and I figured I'd help out. You know what they say, 'Buyer beware.'

There was another message after that said:

But don't do anything stupid like try to find me. I can keep much better tabs on you than you can on me. Sweet dreams!

When Henry saw the title he looked back at Martin.

"I know, right? And the, 'A Friend,' part? How fucked up is that?"

"And you think it's from the person you bought the book of summoning spells from?" Henry asked.

"Isn't it obvious? I mean, I haven't told anyone else about that because A: they'd never believe me and B: It makes me look like a crazy asshole. Which I probably deserve but still . . . this is really fucked up, right? Is this person going to come for me and kill me or something? I just want to forget that this ever happened, y'know?"

Henry nodded. "I understand. Sometimes though, once this door in your life is opened, things can keep coming back to you. You notice things you hadn't before and are drawn to things that most people instinctively avoid."

"Fantastic," Martin said, dropping his head down into his hands. "So what am I supposed to do? Run and hide the rest of my life?"

"Not necessarily," Henry said. "There are--" he was cut off by Martin's phone making an electronic video game sound and vibrating in his hand.

"Sorry," Martin said, reaching out for it. "I thought I turned it to silent."

Before he could take it away Henry looked down at the screen, which had lit up with the new message. Martin drew his hand back when he saw the expression on Henry's face. "What is it?"

"A problem," Henry said, turning the phone to face Martin. There was a new message from, 'A Friend,' which read:

What I said goes double for you, Mr. Churchill. Stay out of my business and I'll stay out of yours. Cheers! :)

The end of "Summer of Sins"

but Lexie Winston & Henry Churchill will return in

"A Shadow Upon The Scenes"

in the second collection

"Fall of Shadows"

ABOUT THE AUTHOR

Thacher E. Cleveland grew up in Montclair, NJ and upstate New York. He moved to Yellow Springs, Ohio after school and stayed for about 15 years, selling books and comics for most of that time, even becoming a co-founder his own shop, Super-Fly Comics & Games. In 2010 he left the retail side of life and relocated first to Chicago and then to Tennessee, where he writes novels (SHADOW OF THE PAST), short stories (The Winston and Churchill supernatural private investigator series) and comics. He can be found online at his website, www.demonweasel.com or Twitter (@demonweasel) or on Tumblr and his writing can be found wherever eBooks are sold.